# THE HARVEY GIRL

ALSO BY DANA STABENOW

The Kate Shugak series

*A Cold Day for Murder*
*A Fatal Thaw*
*Dead in the Water*
*A Cold Blooded Business*
*Play with Fire*
*Blood Will Tell*
*Breakup*
*Killing Grounds*
*Hunter's Moon*
*Midnight Come Again*
*The Singing of the Dead*
*A Fine and Bitter Snow*
*A Grave Denied*
*A Taint in the Blood*
*A Deeper Sleep*
*Whisper to the Blood*
*A Night Too Dark*
*Though Not Dead*
*Restless in the Grave*
*Bad Blood*
*Less Than a Treason*
*No Fixed Line*
*Not the Ones Dead*

The Harvey Girls series

*The Harvey Girl*

The Liam Campbell series

*Fire and Ice*
*So Sure of Death*
*Nothing Gold Can Stay*
*Better to Rest*
*Spoils of the Dead*

✷

The Eye of Isis series

*Death of an Eye*
*Disappearance of a Scribe*
*Theft of an Idol*
*Abduction of a Slave*

✷

*Blindfold Game*
*Prepared for Rage*
*Silk and Song*
*The Collected Short Stories and Essays*
*Alaska Traveler*
*On Patrol With the US Coast Guard*

# THE HARVEY GIRL

## DANA STABENOW

*An Aries Book*

First published in the UK in 2026 by Head of Zeus,
part of Bloomsbury Publishing Plc

Copyright © Dana Stabenow, 2026

The moral right of Dana Stabenow to be identified
as the author of this work has been asserted in accordance with
the Copyright, Designs and Patents Act of 1988.

All rights reserved. No part of this publication may be: i) reproduced
or transmitted in any form, electronic or mechanical, including photocopying,
recording or by means of any information storage or retrieval system without prior
permission in writing from the publishers; or ii) used or reproduced in any way for
the training, development or operation of artificial intelligence (AI) technologies,
including generative AI technologies. The rights holders expressly reserve this
publication from the text and data mining exception as per Article 4(3)
of the Digital Single Market Directive (EU) 2019/790.

This is a work of fiction. All characters, organizations, and events portrayed in this
novel are either products of the author's imagination or are used fictitiously.

9 7 5 3 1 2 4 6 8

A catalogue record for this book is available from the British Library.

ISBN (HB): 9781035916665
ISBN (eBook): 9781035916610

Cover design: Jessie Price | Head of Zeus
Map design (on cover): Mapping Solutions

Printed and bound in Great Britain by Clays Ltd, Elcograf S.p.A.

Bloomsbury Publishing Plc
50 Bedford Square, London, WC1B 3DP, uk
Bloomsbury Publishing Ireland Limited,
29 Earlsfort Terrace, Dublin 2, D02 AY28, Ireland

**HEAD OF ZEUS LTD**
5–8 Hardwick Street
London, EC1R 4RG

To find out more about our authors and books
visit www.headofzeus.com
For product safety-related questions contact productsafety@bloomsbury.com

For honorary niece Dawn Peppinger,
the best research road trip sherpa ever.

A railroad is like a lie – you have to keep building to it to make it stand. A railroad is a ravenous destroyer of towns, unless those towns are put at the end of it and a sea beyond, so that you can't go further and find another terminus. And it is shaky trusting them, even then, for there is no telling what may be done with trestle-work.

Mark Twain

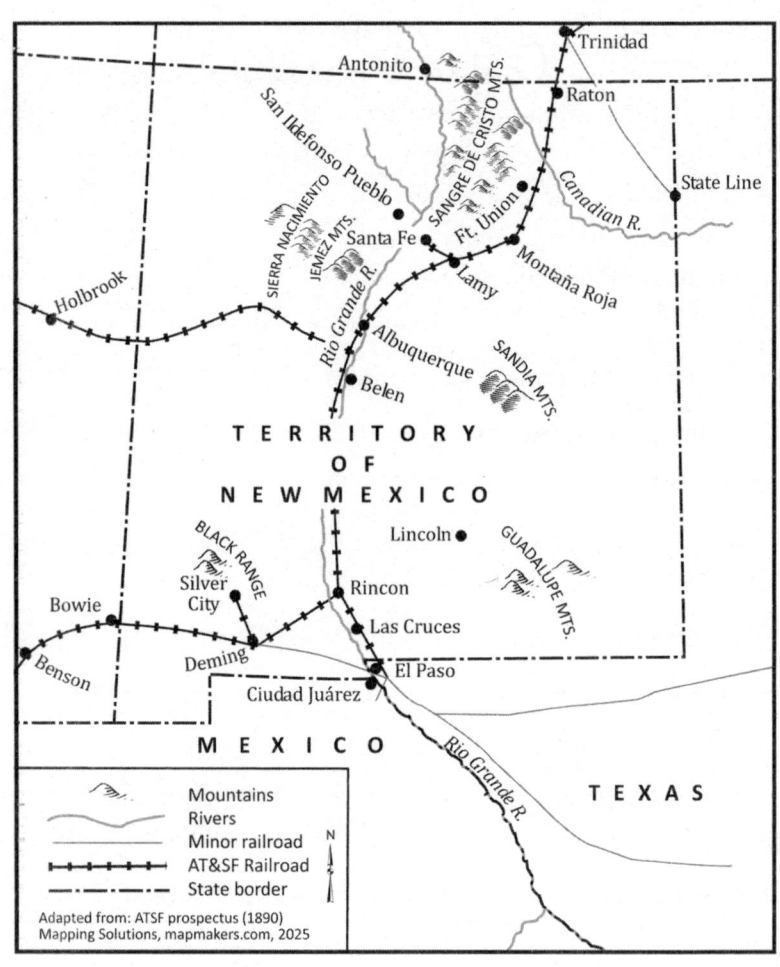

# Cast of Characters

| | |
|---|---|
| Abernathy, Louis | Manager of the Montaña Roja Harvey House |
| Benteen, Algernon, Lt. Col. | CO of 6th Cavalry, Fort Union, New Mexico Territory |
| Berkman, Benjamin | Pinkerton agent |
| Calhoun, Andrew Jackson | Vice-president of Bienville Bank and Trust, Bienville, Mississippi |
| Calhoun, Mary Simpson | Wife of Andrew Jackson Calhoun |
| Clemens, Samuel L. | Author, pen name Mark Twain |
| Dabney, Walter | Indian agent for the New Mexico Territory |
| Doster, Eugene | An agent for the Atchison, Topeka and Santa Fe Railroad |
| Funston, Harry | Conductor or "ramrod" of the Red Mountain Express from Chicago to New Mexico Territory |

| | |
|---|---|
| Funston, Mabel | Wife of Harry Funston, sister of Florence Sellers |
| Gowan, G.W. | George Washington "Wash" Gowan, businessman, made his fortune in barbed wire (Great Western Fence), expanded into oil (Great Western Oil), railroads (Great Western Freight and Transport), and cattle (Gowan Cattle Company) |
| Harvey, Fred | Entrepreneur, restaurateur |
| Higgins, Elizabeth | Harvey Girl, stationed at Montaña Roja |
| Horn, Tom | Pinkerton agent |
| Irwin, Luther | Doctor in Montaña Roja |
| Major, Henrietta | Harvey Girl, stationed at Montaña Roja |
| Masterson, Bartholomew | Pinkerton agent |
| Parker, Bob | Foreman, Gowan Cattle Company |
| Parker, Fred | Sheriff of Montaña Roja |
| Pinkerton, Robert | Co-head of Pinkerton Agency with brother William |

| | |
|---|---|
| Platt, Dudley | Banker and Montaña Roja magistrate |
| Rubio y Castelló, Gabriel Romero | Mexican grandee |
| Sellers, Florence | Harvey Girl, stationed at Montaña Roja |
| Sterling, Ida | Harvey Girl, stationed at Montaña Roja |
| Tate, Aloysius | Pinkerton agent |
| Wright, Clare | Pinkerton agent |

# Prologue

JANUARY 28, 1868

It was less than three years since Lee surrendered to Grant at Appomattox.

It was less than that since the assassination of Abraham Lincoln. He had had five days to enjoy the end of what would prove to be the bloodiest conflict in American history.

In February, the U.S. House of Representatives would impeach President Andrew Johnson, Lincoln's vice-president and successor.

In May, another group of Mercer Girls would arrive in Seattle, coming from Massachusetts to marry lumbermen and fishermen in the Pacific Northwest. Most of them did.

Also in May, Kit Carson, soldier and dime novel hero, would die of an aortic aneurysm.

In July, the Fourteenth Amendment to the U.S. Constitution would be adopted, guaranteeing freed male slaves full U.S. citizenship and all citizens the right to due process of law.

In September, Louisa May Alcott would publish the first part of *Little Women*.

Also in September in Opelousas, Louisiana, more than 250 black Americans would be killed by white vigilantes.

In October, the 6.7 Hayward Earthquake would cause significant damage and many deaths in California.

In October, Robert E. Lee would enjoy his third anniversary as president of Washington University. He continued in that office until his death in 1870.

In November, Ulysses S. Grant would be elected president of the United States.

In November, George Armstrong Custer would attack the Cheyenne at Washita River, killing 103 of them including Chief Black Kettle, and taking fifty of the women as sexual slaves for himself and his officers.

In December, President Johnson would grant unconditional pardons to all Civil War rebels.

Arkansas, Louisiana, Florida, North Carolina, South Carolina, and Alabama would be admitted back into the union with no penalties for seceding in the first place.

It was not a peaceful year or a peaceful country into which to bring a child.

The mother of this child was thirty-five years old and in perfect health. The child was eight months and three weeks along. The doctor, whose hands and apron were covered with the evidence of the five other babies he had already delivered that morning, parted the mother's legs and stuck his head between them. Fingers probed in a manner rough but not prurient to assess how rapidly the birth was progressing. He stood up without bothering to pull the sheet back over the mother's knees. "Everything looks normal, I don't see any problems. Another six hours, perhaps." He shrugged. "Maybe twelve."

The woman pulled the sheet back down over her legs and glared at him but was soon too busy to waste time on anger.

An hour later a healthy baby girl made her appearance in a slick of blood and effluvia. The doctor sniffed at it and exchanged a significant look with the nurse, who put her hand on the woman's forehead for a moment, and nodded at him.

The nurse took the baby from her mother's breast to clean her up and wrap her securely in a soft blanket.

The mother died of childbed fever three hours later.

The child lay in her father's arms, red of face, eyes scrunched tight, rosebud mouth pursed.

"Why not take her home?" William said. Both his sons were there at his request and neither of them was comfortable.

He shook his head. "Your mother would hate her and everything she represented, and the girls would follow their mother's lead. Better she be raised an orphan than that."

He bent his head to kiss the baby's cheek. "You shall not want," he whispered in her ear. "You shall never be hungry or homeless or without support or guidance. I shall be watching over you your whole life long. This I swear to you, and to the spirit of your mother."

He kissed her once more and placed her into the arms of the wet nurse.

"Call her Clare," he said.

## 1

"The engine crew had their hands up
before we even boarded."

*On board the Red Mountain Express
en route to Montaña Roja, New Mexico Territory*

FEBRUARY 5, 1890

WEDNESDAY

"Where are we?" A woman's face, eyes heavy, crowned with a tumble of flattened graying curls. The upper bunk's curtains were at present clutched tightly around her face, omitting any possibility of seeing more, not that he was interested, having seen everything he needed to when she boarded in Chicago. Her daughter, on the other hand, had a figure that would turn Lily Langtry pea green with envy, or would when her stomach settled down from the ride over the Rockies into Raton. He'd had to clean the convenience at the end of the car three times this trip and despite his best efforts the smell lingered.

Ramrodding the Red Mountain Express was not all joy.

The carriage rocked and Harry put one hand on the brass bar running the length of the car. With the other he pulled his watch free and snapped open the case. "We've left the Rockies, Mrs. Perry, and are now rolling out onto the high desert."

"How long until we get to Montaña Roja?" She heard how whiny she sounded and made an attempt at a smile, which almost came off.

His was a wide white slash of genial goodwill. "It's pronounced Moan-tan-ya Ro-hah, ma'am. A little over two hours now." Plus another thirty minutes, he thought, but that shouldn't bother you. He tried to look through the curtains without being obvious about it. "Is there anything I can get for you or your daughter?"

"I can't see anything outside my window." This said fretfully, as befitted an entitled matron going west to join her equally entitled husband, a mine and mill owner and one of Montaña Roja's founders and city fathers. Harry was always on his best behavior with such influential people.

"No, ma'am." He smiled again. "But you are on the correct side of the train to watch the light illuminate the Sangre de Cristo Mountains as the sun rises. I promise you, it is a glorious sight that never fails to please all who see it for the first time."

It was a practiced line that usually inspired something more than a yawn. The curtain across the bunk below twitched aside to reveal the glare of a balding, middle-aged face, a Carnegie man from New York if Harry remembered correctly, which he always did. The Carnegie man said nothing but he didn't have to to make his feelings known. Harry raised his hands in an apologetic shrug, one man to another.

"Mama?" a sleepy voice said from behind the woman. The face vanished with a perfunctory "Thank you, conductor." There was a rustle of blankets and a murmur of voices. He waited hopefully. Alas, the curtain remained firmly closed. Ah well. At least the Carnegie man had vanished, too.

"You're welcome, ma'am." He didn't mean it; all her queries had done was slow him down on the way to the caboose, where a much-needed mug of hot coffee waited for him, but he looked forward as much to the tips at the end of the twenty-four-hour trip as he did the end of the journey itself. Waking people up in the middle of the night did not dispose them toward generosity when deboarding the train.

He made his way through a half dozen more cars unmolested and ended up in the caboose, where a corner had been carved out for a bunk, a table with a bench, and a small pot-bellied stove. The coals were still hot and he threw more on top of them and put the kettle on to boil before sitting down to leaf through the bills of lading on the omnipresent clipboard. A shipment of fresh, canned, and dry goods loaded in Kansas City bound for Fred Harvey Houses from Raton to Montaña Roja to the Fred Harvey warehouse in Lamy and beyond. There was another, much larger shipment bound for Fort Union, although it traveled under seal and the bill of lading didn't specify which goods or how many.

Which told its own tale, he thought, one corner of his mouth curling up with a satisfied smirk.

For the rest there were cars of canned and dried foods and bolts of cloth and leather in varying thicknesses and finishes and hand tools and plows and harrows and threshers and seed and one entire car full of rolls and rolls of barbed wire to be sold by the pound. All were items essential to the farmers and ranchers and miners and the rest of the citizens filling up the burgeoning communities of Santa Fe and Albuquerque and Montaña Roja and other as yet unnamed but soon to be heard from points west.

With another load just like this one coming down the tracks from Chicago tomorrow and every day after that. The American West's maw was empty and bottomless. Its only limit was the Pacific Ocean. The Santa Fe Railroad was on its way there, and Harry Funston was along for the ride as far as it would take him.

The kettle boiled and he added grounds and poured a cup. It was black as oil and tasted like tar. He made a face over his first mouthful but swallowed anyway. His wife, a farm girl, now there was a woman who knew how to make coffee. He'd never bothered learning how. What was the point? There was always a woman willing to take on the care and feeding of a man with money in his pocket, as witness his easy conquest of sweet little Mabel and their burgeoning family of brats. His mother had always said he couldn't have been born so handsome for no reason and he'd always agreed with her.

He checked his watch. They would be coming up on the spur to Colmore shortly. He drained his cup, reached for his cap, settled it to what he knew after serious time spent before his mirror was its most attractive angle. He left the caboose and went forward again, walking steadily but not swiftly as he wouldn't want to arrive too soon. There was a nicety to timing these things.

By the time he reached the sleeping cars the change in the tempo of the rods and wheels had roused a few passengers. A few heads popped out from behind curtains, some yawning, some annoyed that their sleep had been disturbed. "Nothing to worry about," he said in a low voice with a reassuring smile. "Just slowing down for a crossing." From experience he knew he could have said anything, they were slowing down for another train on a cross track, a herd of buffalo, a wildfire, and still they would have done what they did do, which was twitch their curtains closed and go back to sleep.

When he reached the freight car with the correct number, the bell rang the alert, clanging and urgent. The hoghead. Always an alarmist. Sometimes he thought temperamental was in the job description for all train engineers. He only hoped it wasn't loud enough to be heard in the sleeping cars. Changing out the bunks for seats was complicated enough without everyone milling around and getting in his way.

The train shuddered to a halt. He waited until he heard the knock, three long, one short, two long, one short. He grinned. The Army had been good for something other than getting shot at by Indians after all.

He slid the door to one side, having unlocked it on his previous passage down the length of the train. The moon was full up in the sky and flooded the desert plain with light, bleaching the man outside into a ghost wearing a thick jacket, worn jeans, boots without spurs, and a handkerchief tied over his face. His eyes were invisible in the shadow beneath the brim of his hat. He wore a pistol in a holster on his right, opposite a Bowie knife in a leather sheath on the other side.

Funston nodded. "All well?"

A voice muffled by the kerchief. "The engine crew had their hands up before we even boarded."

Funston grinned and jumped down from the car. "You stopped us at the crossing?"

"Just like before, just like always. Ain't our first time."

Didn't he know it. He walked back to the coupler that held the freight car to the car ahead of it and pulled the pin, both clearly illuminated in the moonlight. "Tell them to pull forward."

A whispered command, followed by quick footsteps on gravel. He stood back when the engine pulled the front half of the train forward, past the switch that controlled the second track coming in from the right. He walked back one car, two, three, and pulled another pin.

Sound carried easily in the night, why he didn't know and didn't care, but the second engine approaching from the east was clearly audible. A smaller engine, without the impatient, full-throated growl of their own, no question to anyone who knew trains. He walked forward again and threw the switch so it could move onto the main track. He walked back to the first coupling, where he guided the approaching bolt into the stationary slot. It connected with a satisfying click, and he dropped in the pin. Easy as pie.

He turned. "They're on the hook. Good to go."

Another whispered order and again footsteps. The smaller engine strained and began to move, the three freighters following obediently.

"Like ducklings after their momma," he said with a chuckle.

"Quiet."

He rolled his eyes but did as he was told. They were paying him enough to.

When the third freighter trundled past the switch, heading back the way it came, he walked to the switch stand and returned it to its previous setting.

He fidgeted a little, waiting. He had to get up to the engine to let the hoghead know it was safe to back up and reconnect the train. He pulled his watch and held it up to the moonlight to read the time. Four o'clock in the morning. The whole operation had taken barely twenty minutes and no passengers had appeared to demand what was going on. He should be home in time for breakfast.

A lot of people complained about the new time zones, even seven years later. Not him. He stifled another chuckle. Timing really was everything in a successful robbery and this one had gone off like, well, like clockwork.

There was a crunch of gravel behind him. It startled him into turning quickly.

Too quickly, as he found the man in the act of pulling up his kerchief, but not soon enough to hide his identify.

There was a long moment of silence, followed by a sigh. "You dumb bastard. What did you have to go and do that for?"

"I—I—"

The sound of metal on leather. He backed up, stumbling a little.

"No, I didn't see you, I didn't see anything!" His protesting voice rose to a shout.

"Goddammit. I'm sorry." The other man reached out, spun him around, cupped his chin to pull it up and out of the way, and cut his throat.

Harry's last words were an awful, extended gurgle. He heard it with his own disbelieving ears. What on earth was that sound and what did it mean? A warmth flooded down the front of his chest and the last thing he heard was the other man cursing again.

He was dropped to the ground and left to listen to footsteps crunching on gravel, moving quickly away from him.

His last sight was of the sky, a dense scatter of bright white lights against a black background, the white globe of the full moon, and the faintest hint of a line of light against the eastern horizon of the high desert of the New Mexico Territory.

The last thing he heard was the second engine steaming away.

It was a good fifteen minutes before the engine crew, arms down now that a masked man wasn't pointing the business end of a Colt Peacemaker at them, came back to see what had happened. They found Harry Funston's body sprawled awkwardly across the left-hand track, his spine showing white through the slash across his neck.

"Well, shit," one of them said. He took a quick step to the left and vomited with neatness and dispatch.

His companion, the hoghead and chief engineer, waited for him to be done. "All right, then. Let's load him up so we can get the hell out of here."

They put the conductor in the next freight car down, in two pieces as his head was too heavy for his half-severed spine to bear. When it fell off with an audible tear of skin and crack of bone the first man vomited again. As a testament to his self-control he then picked up the head and put it next to the body.

The hoghead, gifted with even more sangfroid, picked it up and put it in the crook of one of Funston's arms. "It'll roll around otherwise and I don't want to have to chase it up for the sheriff in Montaña Roja." He spat. "Not that that boozer will be of any use whatever in tracking down who did this."

The image of Funston's head rolling around the inside of the freight car made the first man heave a little but he managed not to throw up a third time.

The two of them stood looking at Harry's remains for a moment longer. The moon's light was merciless in illuminating every detail.

"He looks so surprised," the second man said.

"Wouldn't you be?"

"You think he was in on it?"

"Don't you?" He spat again. "On all of them. Pretty slick operation, no flies on these guys. It wouldn't have run as smoothly as it did without at least one of the ramrods in league with the robbers. Recruiting him was probably the first thing they did."

"Then why'd they kill him?"

"I don't know. Maybe he got greedy." The hoghead slid the door closed and they both heard the latch click. "Not our problem."

The first man took a long, deep breath and let it out, and felt a welcome sensation of the world becoming steadier beneath his feet. His was a good job that paid well and he was mostly interested in keeping it. His biggest ambition was to have the hoghead's job one day and given the rapid rate at which the Atchison, Topeka and Santa Fe was laying track that goal was within his reach, and sooner rather than later. Sudden, violent death was a daily occurrence in the American West. Harry Funston's wasn't the first dead body he'd ever seen and wouldn't be the last, but it was the first that had belonged to a person he'd known, even if only on the job. It took some getting used to.

The band of light on the eastern horizon was increasing in height, width, and brilliance, bleaching out the stars but not the moon. The Sangre de Cristo Mountains coalesced out of the dark, at present nothing more than granite ghosts against the still-star-spangled western horizon. But when sunrise happened in the West it happened quickly; by the time the two men returned to the engine the mountains had solidified and begun to take on the deep red color that gave them their name. The only star left in the sky was the morning star, set like a jewel among the mountain peaks.

"Kind of the color of Harry's blood," the hoghead said, engaging the engine.

The other man swallowed hard and looked east, at the sun engulfing the high desert in a great golden flood, lighting the way west for everyone from the robber barons building the railroads to the men and women who would build the communities in their wake.

A much more cheerful prospect.

## 2

Clare decided that Mr. Perkins had divined that the true nature of Mrs. Calhoun was that of a bulldog. He had captured her jowls with particular fidelity to their original.

*Bienville, Mississippi*

FEBRUARY 8, 1890

SATURDAY

The days were warm and humid, which made lying in bed a sweaty chore. Clare had been born in Chicago and educated in Pennsylvania and New York. She did not care for heat, especially when it was hot or humid enough to make her sweat.

But the nights, ah, the nights were different. Cool and dark and breezy, with only glimpses of stars between the tossing tops of bald cypress and live oak, redolent of the scents of magnolia and honeysuckle.

If only one could judge the property owners on landscape and vegetation alone.

The house in which she was currently residing, the home of bank vice-president Andrew Jackson Calhoun and his wife, Mary Simpson Calhoun, was on the outskirts of town. It was a large white mansion, a little too square and a little too squat to be entirely convincing as an example of Greek Revival no matter how many Corinthian columns had been added to its frontage. Before the War Between the States, as the Civil War was known only in the South, the landed gentry had built many such, including this one, which the original owners had lost when they'd been left to pick their own cotton. Calhoun's bank had repossessed it and A.J. Calhoun was fond of boasting of the deal he'd gotten on the property, while his wife Mary hired a maid and trained her to properly announce callers, because America's noovoo richy had no business answering their own doors. The maid's mother became their cook, and if the Calhouns knew that both maid and cook had worked those same positions in that same house before the war at no pay, neither they nor anyone else was so goosh as to say so. Good help was hard to find.

The house sat in the middle of a thickly forested property with a creek cutting across it from the northeast corner to the southwest, probably at some point flowing into the Mississippi. Clare could hear the creek chuckling and chattering over root and stone through her open window. The window was framed by curtains that stirred gently at the merest breath of air. In the distance thunder sounded, a little nearer than it had before.

A sufficient camouflage for any noise she might make. All in all, excellent conditions for infiltration, surveillance, and the collection of evidence. She lay silent, listening. Even three doors down she could hear A.J. snoring. He'd come upstairs at eleven as usual, and as usual at midnight she had woken again to Mary moving stealthily into the bedroom next door to the conjugal one. Mary snored, too, but hers was more a muted gargle than the full-throated foghorn of her husband.

Mary and A.J. resembled their home, both a little square-shaped, both a little squat, and both decked out in the latest fashions whether those fashions became them or not. Mary still wore a bustle with multiple voluminous petticoats beneath her skirts and her corset was laced so tightly that her face was perpetually the red of the ripest tomato. A.J.'s suits were cut so close that gasps for air punctuated the end of every sentence. Clare lived in daily dread of bearing witness to a costume calamity that would bare far more.

She rolled over, snuggled her cheek into an admittedly fine pillow covered by a pillowcase woven of the highest quality linen, and went back to sleep. She woke again at three, being possessed of the ability shared by the best agents to wake at any given hour. The night sky rivaled the color of coal and by now even the owls were heading for their roosts.

She wore a white nightdress trimmed with ripples of lace, a testament to her wholly imaginary life of wealth and privilege. Her robe was black velvet embroidered with jet beads, cut close to her body and ankle-length, useful for flitting about unheard and unobserved. And it had a pocket. She reached inside and pulled out her derringer. It was an elegant example of the gunsmith's art, with a walnut stock, an iron barrel, and a copper-nickel alloy for the trigger guard and the furbelows. A single-shot pistol, loaded with a .45 caliber bullet.

It was dark in her room but her fingers identified and caressed every curve. She could and probably should replace it with a newer model, but they still made ammunition for it and so long as they did, it would be the only personal weapon for her. A gift from her father on her sixteenth birthday. Not that a single gift made up for his too few, too brief appearances in her life.

She shook off the anger that always rose at the thought, and pocketed the derringer and smoothed the skirt of her dressing gown. Her toes peeped out from beneath the hem, bare skin all the better for proceeding noiselessly.

She opened the door to her bedroom and put her ear to the crack. Her hosts' snoring continued undisturbed. The housekeeper's room was downstairs and at the back. A.J.'s office was downstairs, to the right of the front door, kitty-corner from the servant's rooms.

There was a flash of light and the thunder sounded again, both drawing near. She looked at the curtains at her window, which were now flapping in the strengthening breeze.

Perfect.

She stepped into the hall and listened. Still nothing, other than the approaching storm. A sudden gust of wind nearly pulled the door from her hand. She closed it hastily, waiting until the latch clicked, and slipped down the hallway to the head of the stairs. She kept close to the wall as she descended to avoid any creaking steps and ghosted across the polished wooden floor to the door of the office.

Which was locked.

She also carried with her a set of picks. The door was open in a trice. She slipped inside and closed the door carefully behind her.

The office was furnished with more of an eye for wealth than for taste. Heavy bookcases lined two walls. The books that filled the shelves were every one bound in calfskin and gold leaf, and looked as unread as the day they had been placed there. An ornate fireplace adorned the adjacent wall, above which hung a portrait of a man seated, his wife standing behind him with one hand on his right shoulder, set in a gilt frame. She knew them as master and mistress of the house but only because they had been her hosts for the past week, and they had not failed to drop the name of the artist and bemoan the time wasted on their sittings at least four or five times during Clare's visit. "Such a perfectionist, Mr. Perkins!" Mrs. Calhoun had said with a simper. "He insisted an extra sitting was necessary so as to catch the true nature of my expression."

Lightning flashed outside the window and in that momentary illumination Clare decided that Mr. Perkins had divined that the true nature of Mrs. Calhoun was that of a bulldog. He had captured her jowls with particular fidelity to their original. What was more, she bore a remarkable resemblance to her husband, at least on canvas. Remove his muttonchops and her frizette and it would have been difficult to tell them apart. Clare wondered if Mr. Perkins' skill was limited to one face and one face only. On the evidence, she thought it possible.

The hearth was framed by two twin Oriental jars painted a red that was almost brown beneath a design of white flowers that looked suspiciously like the magnolias on the trees outside. Probably not the Tang Dynasty Chinese porcelain Mr. Calhoun had boasted them to be, then.

A heavy mahogany desk sat in front of the window overlooking the driveway, its gravel meticulously raked by the groundsman before he went to bed. The desk's surface was neat, papers in tidy piles, pen and ink with no messy drips defiling its own polished wooden stand, a round crystal paperweight arranged at top center just so.

She made no attempt to examine the paperwork. That task had been undertaken on a previous night and been productive of nothing in particular. She didn't care how he'd done it anyway. She only wanted proof that he had, which meant recovering the stolen money in his hands. Tonight's entertainment was the culmination of a plan that had been devised with precisely that goal in mind.

She swept the paperwork across the desk, much of it fluttering into the air to scatter across the floor. She pulled a vial from her pocket, uncorked it and dribbled the contents in a trail over the chair and desk and the papers.

She stopped to listen and heard nothing but wind and thunder. She corked the vial and stowed it away. She went to the double glass doors behind the desk that opened onto the brief terrace that fronted the driveway. Behind them the thunder sounded again and much nearer. Good. The breeze had increased to gusts. Even better.

She opened the doors and flung them wide, where, as she had hoped, they were caught by the gusts and began to bang against the front of the house. One of the panes obligingly shattered. A flash of lightning illuminated the house and grounds, for an instant making them look as ghostly as she was pretending to be.

She whipped around to snatch up the crystal paperweight and with all her might threw it at one of the fake Oriental vases standing next to the fireplace. There was a satisfactory crash that rivaled the thunder, and bits and pieces of red and white ceramics peppered the skirt of her robe. She found the paperweight and threw it again, this time directly at the very bad portrait of Andrew Jackson Calhoun, vice-president of the Bienville Bank and Trust, the man she intended to prove thief and murderer this night. Not forgetting his wife, Mary, who, Clare was equally certain, was his accomplice in the crime.

She heard voices from upstairs, knocked the pen and ink stand from the desk and darted from the room, pausing only to pull the door closed behind her, and melted into the shadows beneath the staircase. Panicked footsteps sounded in the hallway above and then pounded down the stairs, and she watched as Calhoun skidded across the polished wooden floor to the door of his office. His hand was shaking so badly he couldn't get the key into the lock, which gave his wife time to follow him downstairs.

"Andrew! What on earth is going on!" Her footsteps sounded overhead and the stairs creaked beneath her weight.

"For god sakes, woman, stay upstairs! Didn't you hear the noise? The storm has broken the office doors!"

He got the key in the lock at last and opened the door to see the destruction therein. A rising shriek spiraled up into the night. "What have I done! Oh, what have I done!"

"Andrew!" In her haste Mrs. Calhoun nearly tripped and fell over the bottom step and uttered a startled cry. Mr. Calhoun spun in place and started forward, his arms held out. Mrs. Calhoun stumbled trying to regain her balance. They collided in the middle of the hallway and went sprawling.

Clare put her hand to her mouth and made a heroic effort not to laugh out loud.

Mr. Calhoun's voice rose in a wail. "His ghost! His ghost has come back to haunt me for my sins!"

Mrs. Calhoun was less susceptible to atmosphere. "Don't be silly, Andrew, there are no such things as ghosts." She pulled him into her arms and patted his head. "He's buried and gone, my dear. He shall bother us no more with his incessant talk of outspending our income and overdue bills."

"But his ghost!" He raised a trembling finger and pointed. "There is blood on my desk, Mary! Like there was on my pillow! And on my suit!"

"Nonsense, my dear sir! This is all in your imagination, to be sure!"

"But the blood, Mary! It's there!" Calhoun jumped to his feet. "What if the box is gone? I must check to see!"

Her voice sharpened. "No, Andrew! We agreed! We go nowhere near it for a year, until all the talk has died down and it is safe!"

"No, no, I must see with my own eyes!" He fumbled with the bolt on the massive front door and flung it wide, where a gust of wind immediately slammed it against the table standing next the wall. There was the sound of splintering wood and shattering marble and a corresponding moan from Mrs. Calhoun. "My console! My beautiful console!"

But by then her husband had vanished into the night. Lightning cracked and thunder boomed almost on cue. Really, this was better than one of Vernon Lee's Gothic romances.

Mrs. Calhoun finally managed to get to her feet and staggered into the office, from where Clare heard a cry of anguish. "My vase! My beautiful vase!"

Clare pulled on her shoes. A floorboard creaked behind her and a flash of lightning revealed the busty black cook and the maid, a paler, waif-like antithesis of her mother. They stared at her, unblinking, while all three of them listened to Mrs. Calhoun's lamentations. After a few moments of this the cook touched her daughter on the arm and nodded at the door into the kitchen. They vanished behind it without a word.

No succor or comfort for their employer, it seemed.

Clare went after Calhoun. There was no hurry. She knew where he was going.

As she stepped outside the heavens opened up and she was drenched before she had crossed the lawn into the trees. Ahead of her she could hear someone crashing through the brush, the breath sobbing out of him in great pants. He ran headlong into an oak, rebounded and staggered around it, half dazed, only to impact a magnolia. Undeterred he spat a flower out of his mouth and kept going. She followed at a discreet distance but there was no danger of losing him and no danger at all of being heard by him. An elephant would have made less noise. At least he was frightening off all the wildlife that might be in the area.

He splashed into the creek at last, as wet to the skin as she was by the warm rain sheeting down, although it was beginning to ease and the lightning and thunder were already moving off. She blinked her lashes free of rain and saw his dark figure outlined against the surface of the water. He was bent over, his hands thrust beneath its surface, his hands scrabbling feverishly at the creek bottom. She could hear him mumbling to himself. "Where is it? Where is it?"

His voice rose again to a moan. "It has to be here! It has to be here!"

No answer, not from the murdered man Calhoun was addressing and certainly not one from Clare.

He sloshed forward, clawing again at the gravel. His left hand caught on something and he grabbed at whatever it was with a cry. He tugged and lost his grip and sat down in running water up to his waist. A branch caught by the water swollen by rain struck him in the face and he surged up again with an oath and went back to tugging. Whatever he had hold of was not coming up easily and he bent double over the task, upon which his trousers ripped right down the seam. He had not waited to don his drawers before he pulled them on. Clare kept her eyes fixed firmly on the back of his head.

He grunted and strained and finally, with a yell of triumph, he pulled his objective free, a large, flat stone that looked as if it had been taken from the terrace at the back of the house.

He slung it aside and went back to feeling around beneath the water, tugging and swearing and tugging some more. Finally he planted his feet and really put his back into it and at last it gave way, so suddenly that he lost his balance and staggered backward and sat down again. The water rushed around him, unheeding.

He sat where he was, clutching his prize to his breast, sobbing for real now, the tears coursing down his cheeks in amounts that rivaled the water pouring down the creek.

It was a box, eighteen inches long, about a foot deep and perhaps eight inches in height.

She stepped out onto the creek bank and down into the water. His back stiffened when he heard her but he wouldn't turn around. His voice quavered when he spoke. "Is it you, Horace? Ha-have you come for me?"

"No, I've come for this," Clare said, and reached around him to take the box. It was made of metal, thin but sturdy, fastened securely with a small brass padlock. It wasn't heavy but it might be just heavy enough.

At first he wouldn't let go, and then he did so all at once. His head and shoulders bowed, still crying, the water of the creek swollen by the rain swirling and eddying around him. She tucked the box under her arm and put her other hand beneath his elbow. "Come now, Mr. Calhoun. Let's get you out of the creek and onto dry land."

He let her pull him up without comment and plodded after her to the bank. Once there, he gaped at her. "Who? What? Mrs. Hammond? What?"

She laughed. "I'm afraid it's Miss Wright. Miss Clare Wright. How do you do, Mr. Calhoun. I work for the Pinkerton Detective Agency."

He gasped, took a step backward, tripped and fell back into the creek.

After sunrise, once again in dry clothes and packed and ready to go, she joined her fellow agents in the office downstairs. Mr. and Mrs. Calhoun had been relocated to the town jail.

She nodded at them. "Did you open it?"

"No, we thought we'd wait for you." Berkman, very solemn, and Tate rolled his eyes.

"Nice of you." She picked the padlock and unlatched the box. The contents were wrapped in several layers of oilskin, but once they were opened it was all there, if slightly damp. "Should we count it?"

"Should we take it and head for Mexico?"

Berkman and Clare gave Tate reproving glances. He shrugged and grinned. "Worth a try."

They counted it, each of them, one after the other. "We're all agreed?" Clare said. "Two hundred ninety-nine thousand seven hundred and fifty dollars?"

"Agreed." Berkman glanced around. "I expect this house will cover the difference."

Clare shrugged, packing the money back into the box, watched by Tate with a yearning expression. "It's mortgaged and from what I overheard over the last week they owe everybody." She rummaged in the desk for pen and paper and wrote out a receipt, which the three of them signed. She replaced it in the box, latched it, and replaced the padlock.

"We'll turn this over to the sheriff and alert the bank headquarters in Memphis," Berkman said. "Want me to send him a telegram that you're on your way?"

She yawned and stretched. It had been a long night. She would have liked a few more hours of sleep. "I suppose."

"You suppose rightly. The B's wanted you in Chicago yesterday."

The B's were how the employees privately referred to the two Pinkerton brothers, William and Robert, or Bill and Bob. "Did they say why?"

Berkman shook his head. "The telegram said urgent."

She rolled her eyes. "They always say it's urgent. Did somebody die?"

"Well." He cocked an eyebrow. "Somebody did here."

He had her there.

"I got you a ticket on the noon train. Memphis and then Chicago."

"Please tell me it's a sleeper."

He grinned, and Tate laughed, and she groaned.

It was late afternoon when she disembarked in Chicago and went directly to the two rooms she called home. Rented from a widow with more house than her late husband's pension could support, the flat had its own entrance, a tiny kitchen off the living room, and an even tinier bath off the bedroom, all three of which added considerably to the rent. She switched on the gas light and prepared to change identities.

In Bienville, as always, she had dressed to suit the case, becoming one with her immediate environment. In this instance she had imitated the carpetbaggers who had swarmed into the South after the Civil War. They had pilfered property and fortune by means mostly foul and were now trying to live up to the standards of the Astors and Vanderbilts and Rockefellers, or at least as those families appeared in the society pages of New York City newspapers.

Her fingers went to work on too many buttons, bows, and strings. The heavily fringed mantle, the even more heavily flounced skirt, the multiple petticoats, the bustle, the corset fell to the floor and were kicked into a corner. Finally her skin was once again free to breathe. She belted on a light cotton wrapper patterned with pink roses and sat down at the table to stare at the mirror hung on the wall behind it. It was part of the ritual that ended every case, a slow, deliberate reintroduction to herself.

The woman looking back at her was in her early twenties, with clear skin like polished ivory and hair that looked dark in the light of the gas lamp but gleamed auburn in the direct sun. Her hands began searching for the pins securing the switch that formed the top of the elaborate chignon and she sighed with relief as one by one they stopped digging into her scalp. She undid the braid of her own hair, ran her fingers through it to loosen the strands, and then took a brush to it, at first back from her face and then standing up to brush it forward. She tossed it back again. The thick glossy unrestrained swath reached halfway down her back, freed to regain its natural wave.

Her brows were arched over eyes a deep, dark blue. Her nose was straight, her mouth a wide cupid's bow, and a jaw that when examined too closely might be a little too firm for beauty. Not that many people ever looked that far up, men and women both, as she had been blessed with a good figure, although mercifully not one as voluptuous as the sketches of Charles Dana Gibson in *Life* magazine. Breasts and hips that large could only get in the way of the physical exertions often necessary in pursuing a case to a successful conclusion.

She smiled involuntarily, revealing white, even teeth, a product of natural good health, a good diet and good medical care from birth, and personal vanity. She had a horror of rotten and missing teeth and was determined to take every preventative measure available to her to avoid acquiring either.

"Hello, Clare," she said to her reflection. "How nice to see you again."

She had purchased a sausage sandwich and an apple and carried them home with her from the station and, clearing a space on the table, tucked in. When the last crumb was gone and the apple eaten right down to its core, she cleared the table again, found pencil and paper, and settled in to write her report.

She thought the B's would enjoy it.

## 3

"How would you like to become a Harvey Girl, Miss Wright?"
"I'm sure I wouldn't like it at all, sir."

*Chicago*

FEBRUARY 10, 1890

MONDAY

"Report."
She kept her face expressionless and her voice even. "I dropped off my written report with your secretary this morning." It was sitting on the desk right in front of him. From where she sat she could read the label she herself had affixed to the envelope.

"I know, I read it. Embellish."

The portrait on the wall behind him was by a better artist than the one retained by the Calhouns and emphasized the similarities between father and sons. Stocky, balding, a dark, well-trimmed beard, a long, straight nose, steady blue eyes beneath heavy brows. Those eyes of the living man were fixed on her face at the moment. She met them without flinching. She was long past being intimidated by anyone named Pinkerton. "Which details in particular would you like embellished, sir?"

"The one that interests me most is that you were supposed to be here the day before yesterday."

"I exercised my own judgement by remaining in Mississippi to complete my previous assignment, sir," she said coolly. "Which I did, including apprehending the murderers of Horace Hallett and recovering all but $250 of the $300,000 stolen from the Bienville Bank and Trust."

His eyebrows went up. "Murderers?" He emphasized the plural.

"Murderers," she said firmly. "His wife distracted Hallett so that Calhoun could attack him from behind. They were both confessing to the sheriff as I departed, each of them trying to blame the other. No love lost there." She thought of the body of the clerk, an inoffensive little man with a trace of hair on his upper lip that he had tried hard to coax into a mustache. Like everything else about his life, it was aspirational, right down to the pitifully shiny boots on his feet, as if he'd tried to polish away the cheapness and lack of style. A loyal and faithful employee of Bienville Bank and Trust, to the point of working late when it was required of him, and it was of course late at night when he was struck down in his own office so the Calhouns could burgle the safe.

Robert Pinkerton couldn't hide his disdain. "They couldn't have been all that intelligent if you managed to convince them they were being haunted by the clerk's ghost."

"I did my homework before I, ah, arranged to become a guest in their home, sir. They both attended séances by a medium who lived in the area, a woman called Ayres, who is well known to Mississippi law enforcement."

"Ah yes, you 'arranged to become a guest.' By falling off a horse?"

"I wasn't injured, sir."

"But they thought you were."

"That was the point of falling off the horse in their front yard. Sir."

He tapped her report with his finger. "A satisfactory conclusion to the case, Miss Wright. If your methods were a trifle unorthodox."

She relaxed so that her spine touched the back of the chair without actually leaning on it. "Thank you, sir."

He looked over her shoulder at the man sitting in one of the chairs flanking the fireplace. Pinkerton hadn't introduced them when she had arrived but she had felt his attention during the entire interrogation. "Mr. Harvey?"

She turned to see the other man rise and come forward. He was taller and slimmer than Pinkerton and had more hair, although it was graying, especially the mustache and the goatee. He was plainly but elegantly attired in a tailored black three-piece suit, white shirt and soft black tie, a modest gold chain disappearing into his watch pocket.

He paused before the desk and smiled at her.

Without consciously willing it, she rose to her feet and smiled back.

"Fred Harvey, Miss Wright. Miss Clare Wright, is it not?"

"It is." She hesitated, and then held out her hand. His was warm and dry and strong without trying to crush hers, and releasing her before the gesture became either a caress or an effort at domination. "That would be Fred Harvey, of the Fred Harvey Houses?"

His smile broadened. "It would indeed."

"I have dined at your Englewood Station establishment several times, sir."

"I hope you enjoyed yourself?"

"The food and service both were of a quality I have seldom experienced, sir. Especially for sixty cents a meal."

He sat down in the chair next to hers. She resumed her seat and looked at Pinkerton, who waved at Harvey to continue.

"I understand you are twenty-two years of age, Miss Wright."

"That is correct."

"Not married or engaged? No children?"

She shook her head. "No family at all." She didn't look at Pinkerton. "I'm an orphan, as it happens. I was born in Chicago to unnamed parents. There was a patron who placed me first in a dame cottage in Pennsylvania and then in Vassar."

"Vassar, really. And did you matriculate?"

"I did, with a degree in education."

"Impressive." He glanced at Pinkerton. "Why become a detective instead of a teacher?"

"A detective's salary is some four times the salary of the average teacher. On occasion supplemented by a percentage of the recovery as a bonus. And…" She hesitated.

"Yes?"

"I don't think I'm suited for a life lived within four walls."

He looked amused. "If what I have just heard is a correct accounting of your activities this past month, I would have to agree with you." He gave her a shrewd look. "And I don't expect you've told your employer all of it." He was silent but not long enough for her to become uncomfortable with his intuition. In fact she hadn't told the whole story but neither he nor Pinkerton needed to know that. "I'm told you've worked at Pinkerton's for two years. With some success, as I've just heard."

"Mr. Pinkerton is too kind."

"I doubt it." He smoothed his trouser leg and sat back in his chair. "How would you like to become a Harvey Girl, Miss Wright?"

She cast down her eyes. "I'm sure I wouldn't like it at all, sir."

"Miss Wright!" Pinkerton said.

But Harvey laughed. "Indeed, with my new understanding of your adventures in detection, I can understand why." He sobered and she raised her head to meet his earnest look. "I'm in serious difficulty, Miss Wright, and I believe you can help me find my way out of it."

She spread her hands. "It's what we are here for, Mr. Harvey." She could almost hear Pinkerton purr.

All traces of humor vanished. "As you may or may not know, the Harvey Houses are affiliated with the Atchison, Topeka and Santa Fe Railroad."

"Of course."

"We ship all our supplies via their lines. Fresh produce, eggs, cheese, meats, fish and shellfish, dry goods, cutlery, pots and pans, flatware, glassware, tableware, linens…" He shook his head. "Consumables of course must be replenished daily. There is never a train that travels to, say, the New Mexico Territory without at least one car filled with supplies for the Montaña Roja or La Castañeda or El Ortíz. Or to replenish the warehouse in Lamy." He saw her expression. "Harvey Houses in the New Mexico Territory, Miss Wright, along the ATSF route."

"I see. And the difficulty?"

He gave a heavy sigh. "The trains are being robbed."

She remained silent. There was a train robbery in the American West reported daily in the newspapers and not only in the New Mexico Territory. That the ATSF had been a victim was not exactly news.

"Three times over the last year, well, four times as of last Wednesday, the Red Mountain Express has been stopped between Trinidad, Colorado and Montaña Roja, New Mexico, each on the night of the full moon. Each time the hoghead—pardon me, the engineer of the train—saw an obstruction made of lengths of timber on the tracks ahead and stopped the train in time to avoid running into it, which would have put it at risk of coming off the tracks." He looked at her to ensure that she understood. "The obstruction was always on a long straight stretch of track so that in the light of the full moon he had plenty of time to see it and bring the train to a halt. There was never any danger of derailment, which could have resulted in injury to crew and passengers.

"The place where each train was halted was also just before or just after a branch line intersected with the high iron." He saw their expressions. "I apologize again. Every industry has its own jargon, does it not? High iron refers to the main line of every route. The branch lines or the spurs lead from the main line to smaller towns and business concerns such as mines, mills, and lumberyards. At any rate, the robberies take place in the ideal location for another engine to be waiting, obviously by design. The ramrod, or conductor, is forced at gunpoint to uncouple the freight cars, after which the robbers' engine latches on and takes them off down the intersecting line."

He sat back again, frowning. "The conductor is the highest authority on board the train. He is responsible for seeing that each car gets to its destination and that freight and passengers are offloaded at the correct station. Each of the four trains that were robbed was operating under the authority of the same conductor, one Harry Funston. It seemed almost too certain that the conductor must be involved." He sighed.

"Have you examined his background, his circumstances? Was he showing signs of unexplained affluence? Buying luxury goods, building a larger house than his salary would cover..." She shrugged. "Being seen on the town with a lady not his wife?"

"Miss Wright!"

Harvey and Clare both ignored Pinkerton's expostulation.

"Not that we could find, and I assure you, we looked. If he was being paid off, it didn't show in any of his accounts or in his behavior. A modest man in a rented house close to the station in Montaña Roja. He conducts the Red Mountain Express to Chicago, overnights, and conducts the next day's southbound train to Montaña Roja. In Chicago he spends the night at the Englewood Station hotel." A trace of frustration crossed his face. "It has to have been him. He is the only common denominator in all four robberies. Other than the full moon and a hundred and fifty miles of track."

"When does he, er, conduct his next train?"

Harvey glanced at Pinkerton. "Yes, well, therein lies my difficulty."

"Which is?"

"He's dead," he said bluntly. "His throat was cut by one of the men who robbed the last train. This one just south of Raton."

The silence following this bald statement lasted long enough to hear the ticking of the clock sitting on the mantelpiece.

"Which would argue, surely, Mr. Harvey, that the, ah, conductor in question was perhaps not in the pay of the robbers after all."

Harvey shook his head. "Or that he crossed them somehow and this was how they chose to deal with the betrayal."

"Certainly another possibility." Clare glanced at Pinkerton and back at Harvey. "Why do you come to us with this, Mr. Harvey, and not the ATSF?"

He frowned at his feet. "They are inclined to see train robberies as the price of doing business, Miss Wright. It is, I regret to say, a commonly held attitude among most owners of railroads." He looked up to meet her eyes. "It is not mine."

"I see." She clasped her hands and sat back. "What is it you would like the Pinkertons to do, Mr. Harvey? Find Mr. Funston's murderer? Find the robbers? Or find your stolen goods?"

Harvey looked at Pinkerton. "All three, preferably." He looked back at her. "I knew this man, Miss Wright."

Which made the injury sting all the worse, she thought, and not for sentimental reasons. Harvey wasn't sad; he was angry.

"Even if he was guilty, he wasn't the mastermind behind these robberies. At best he was a necessary minion, who did what he was told."

Until perhaps he didn't, Clare thought. "I see. And how is it you think I might help?" She remembered his previous question. "Oh."

He gave her an approving nod. "Exactly."

"As a Harvey Girl, I would hardly have freedom of movement to investigate."

"You will be assigned to the Montaña Roja Harvey House, a hundred miles south of Raton in the New Mexico Territory. It serves lunch and dinner and operates a newsstand." He hesitated, giving her a long look. "Ideally, what I want you to do is find these criminals before they corrupt another ramrod, use him to steal more from us, and then kill him, too."

She appreciated the distinction he made between robbery and murder. She began to like Fred Harvey.

His gaze was straight and unflinching. "It won't be easy. You must appear to be the genuine article. Mr. Pinkerton and I have been discussing your cover. My manager, Tom Gable, will, ah, finesse your application, but you will have to go through the same month's training every Harvey Girl does." He raised his hands. "Are you up for it?"

Again, she didn't look at Pinkerton. "Will I earn the same pay as every other Harvey Girl? On top, of course, of my salary as a Pinkerton agent?"

She heard Pinkerton harrumph deep in his throat, but this time Harvey laughed. "More than that, Miss Wright. Mr. Pinkerton and I have already discussed this, and we are agreed that Pinkerton, on top of their usual fee, will take a ten percent finder's fee for the value of all the goods recovered as a result of your investigation. Provided it is successful, of course."

Pinkerton, perhaps tired of being ignored, harrumphed again. They looked at him. "You won't be entirely on your own, Miss Wright."

"No?"

"No. I have hired some, well, you might call it freelance assistance. They are already in place in Montaña Roja."

Clare felt a sense of foreboding. "Who?"

He told her, and she closed her eyes briefly. When she opened them again she noticed Pinkerton looking particularly smug.

He really must think she would get herself killed this time.

# 4

"They can run faster than this train
if they've a mind to."

*Montaña Roja, New Mexico*

### March 19, 1890

### Wednesday

They came down out of the tallest mountains Clare had ever seen onto a plain that had no end beneath a sky so clear it was almost colorless.

She was the first in the Pullman car to wake and slipped down the narrow corridor to use the convenience and was dressed long before the conductor appeared to turn the beds back into seats. She closed her bag and left it inside the door at the rear of the car and stepped outside. The cold, dry air was invigorating, and the car was far back enough from the engine to spare her from sparks and soot and engine noise, although the clack of pistons and metal wheels on metal tracks could never be wholly ignored. She moved from side to side on the tiny platform, trying to see as much and as far as possible. Her eyes felt stretched over distances that felt limitless, and in spite of reminding herself, repeatedly, that this was just another job, she couldn't stem the rise of excitement, of anticipation, of sheer wonder the landscape inspired.

Born in Chicago, raised in rural Pennsylvania, educated in rural New York State, during her professional life thus far Clare had been assigned to work in communities east of the Mississippi. She was as new to the American West as were most of her fellow passengers, and had been as mesmerized as any of them by the geographical wonders on display between Chicago and the New Mexico Territory. She had found the vast plains oddly frightening in their endless lack of feature other than the occasional isolated farmstead, the Rocky Mountains had struck her speechless with their massive grandeur, and now this limitless high desert unrolled before her beneath an equally limitless sky.

It was in equal parts terrifying and magnificent, and it was undeniably thrilling. She gripped the thin iron railing and leaned forward so as not to allow a moment to escape her notice.

The door opened behind her and closed again. She looked around to see a tall man dressed in a black three-piece suit and a low-crowned beaver hat. In his late thirties, she thought, he was beardless, revealing a firm jaw and a stern mouth. Dark hair was swept back over a broad forehead and seemed to stay there without recourse to some stinky pomade. He had thick straight brows that nearly met over deep-set brown eyes and a long, strong nose. His attire was fashionable without being fussy and had obviously been tailored to fit. Other than that it was not designed to draw attention.

They had that in common.

"Ma'am. I hope you don't mind the company." His voice was deep and steady. He didn't sound as if he were asking permission.

She inclined her head and turned to face outward again. "The view is free to all, sir."

"For those of us who have the wit to appreciate it."

He came to stand next to her and she could sense his interest.

She was well aware of what he saw, a young woman in her early twenties with enough money to dress respectably if not fashionably. Her short jacket was serviceable and matched the gored skirt, both made from a light gray wool. The hem of the skirt stopped at her ankles, revealing half boots of what had been good black leather, brave beneath a layer of polish. A thin frill of white lace showed over the collar of her jacket and a black-and-white feather was the only decoration on a flat black cap. This was held firmly in place by two plain iron hatpins above the heavy braid coiled at the nape of her neck. She wore no earrings or brooches and her black gloves were plain. Nothing was new, thanks to a productive trip to the clothing store in Chicago that had a large back room filled with racks of used clothing in styles going back before the war. Hers was the carefully curated image of a young, unmarried woman of few means, not entirely destitute but someone who lived close to the bone. In short, the perfect candidate for a job within the Fred Harvey enterprise.

"What is your destination, ma'am, if I may ask?"

She smiled again, more fully this time, taking care to be only polite, not inviting. "You may, sir. I am to join the staff at the Montaña Roja Harvey House."

"Ah. Is this your first House?"

She allowed her eyebrows to rise. "You are familiar with the brand, I see."

"I am. Indeed, I am one of Mr. Harvey's most loyal customers." His smile was quick and conscious of its own charm. Few women had said no to this man, and the realization put her on her guard.

"Have you visited the West before, ma'am?"

She shook her head. "This is my first time crossing the Mississippi." She turned back to the view. "I had no idea."

"No one does, until they see it for the first time. And some, not even then." He leaned against the railing next to her, close enough to ensure she couldn't miss his presence, not close enough to pretend a familiarity that didn't exist. "It is almost another world, isn't it? I promise you, that feeling does not change over time."

"Familiarity does not breed contempt?"

He chuckled. "It does not. Never take it for granted, Miss—"

"I was just thinking of how the first people here must have thought they'd never see water again."

"It's here, you just have to find it. And carry some with you while you're looking."

She smiled. "In his book, Captain Marcy writes of natural caverns full of water."

"So you've read the good captain, have you? Yes, there are such caves across New Mexico and Arizona both, and

I've heard·tell into California as well. They were used by the Indians during their travels. But I don't think they are something one just stumbles upon."

"Are you a permanent resident of the West, sir?"

"I am now. I have business interests in the Territory, and I just built a house in Montaña Roja." He raised his hat. "Wash Gowan, at your service."

She admired his skill. She would be rude now not to share her name, which would not be in keeping with the persona she had created for this investigation. "Clare Wadsworth, at yours."

"And where are you from, Miss Clare Wadsworth?" He paused, giving her time to correct the "miss" if necessary.

She said only, "New York, sir."

He was mildly surprised. "Indeed? Fred usually hires farm girls from Kansas. Or Missouri, or Iowa."

"You know Mr. Harvey, sir?"

"I know him well. I help supply the House in which you will be working. Have you met him yet?"

She shook her head. "Mr. Harvey was traveling when I went into training. I've met Mr. Gable, of course."

"You will. Fred makes it a point to meet all his employees. New York City or New York state?"

"Saratoga Springs."

"Ah. A beautiful town. You have family there?"

"I did."

He waited for her to elaborate. She didn't. He opened his mouth to pursue the topic when she pointed. "Oh, look!"

A herd of animals crested a rise of the prairie and vanished down the other side. She had just enough time to see the distinctive curved horns and the white rumps.

"Pronghorn antelope," Gowan said.

She let out a long breath. "How lovely."

"Tasty, too," he said.

She gave him a reproving look and he laughed. "But first you have to catch them. They can run faster than this train if they've a mind to."

"Really?"

He nodded. "I've seen them do it. If somebody could get a saddle on one they'd win every race at Saratoga."

He was going to say more when the whistle blew, a long blast that obscured anything he might have to say. He waited for it die away. "I believe we must be coming into Montaña Roja, Miss Wadsworth."

"Well, then, I must fetch my bag. Excuse me, Mr. Gowan."

He raised his hat. "Of course."

She could feel his eyes on her as she went through the door.

By neither word nor deed did she reveal that she had known who he was from the moment he appeared on the platform, and before, when she saw him board the train in Kansas City.

She checked the hidden pocket she had sewn into her skirt, feeling for the reassuring weight of her derringer and the little notebook and pencil that never left her person when she was on a case. The rose-patterned carpet bag, of good quality but now worn and faded, perfectly suited her cover identity. She snapped it open to check the contents, which contained a neatly folded stack of two uniforms, a spare shirt and another dressier shirt, both white, underthings, and a smaller bag for personal items. Nothing that would not bear close examination by anyone who cared to look. At most she could have been accused of extreme tidiness.

Gowan passed her in the aisle and raised his hat. She acknowledged his salute with a polite nod.

She was not prepared to take Mr. Gowan at face value, however. For one thing, he was far too attractive, and the Quaker schools taught their students to read from the Bible. She cast a long, thoughtful glance after Mr. Gowan, and 2 Corinthians, chapter 11, verse 14, came to mind. An unfair assessment at a first and admittedly brief meeting, perhaps.

Perhaps.

The locomotive puffed into the station and screeched to a halt, the passenger cars positioned perfectly between the ends of the solid wooden platform and the freight cars precisely aligned with the warehouses built next to the tracks. Clare hung back to watch the rest of the passengers debark, which process oftentimes resembled more of a stampede than a dignified exit. She noticed Gowan was among the first off, and through the window she watched him join a fellow passenger, perhaps a traveling companion, a slim, slight, stooped gentleman with a bushy thatch of reddish hair turning white and an equally bushy mustache that curved from his upper lip all the way around his mouth. You could scrub the floor with that mustache. He wore a black suit and a white hat with a black band and took Gowan's hand and his own good time descending from the car to the platform.

There was something familiar about him but before she could decide where she knew him from, he was quickly superseded by the mother and three small children who had occupied the bunk below hers. None of them had gotten much sleep. The mother, a plump, flustered woman whose jacket buttons were all in the wrong holes and whose hat was sliding off the side of her head, darted first after one child and then another as they each took off in four different directions at once. When a man her age and same general shape thrust his way through the crowd on the platform, she fell on his chest and burst into tears. With cries of "Daddy!" the children homed in like the hands of a compass pointing north. As the crowd swallowed them up Clare noticed that the ruffle matching the mother's jacket had ripped free of her skirt's hem, trailing behind her like a bedraggled tail.

She collected her bag and walked up the aisle. The man in front of her was in his early thirties, pale and sweaty, with protuberant eyes that looked hunted or haunted or perhaps both. He was dressed with that particular lack of panache emblematic of the traveling salesman, all flash and no style, a faded black suit coat worn over a loud green-and-gold checked waistcoat and a pair of brown corduroy trousers worn white at the seat and knees. Everything looked one size too small. The toes of his shoes were scuffed and his brown homburg was covered with soot. A sample case tied shut with a length of twine was clutched to his chest with both arms and his gaze darted across the crowd as if he were looking for someone. Even from behind he smelled as if he had started drinking in Kansas City.

The crowd had somehow doubled in size, while at the same time the hubbub attendant on such gatherings had quieted almost to a hush. She cast an inadvertent look behind her to see who or what had cast such a spell. She was the last person to exit the car, and when she faced forward again, saw that the crowd had cleared a space between the traveling salesman, who was teetering dangerously on the bottom step of the carriage, and a shadow standing at the other end of the cleared space. The shadow stepped forward, resolving itself into a short man in a smart black derby. His hand swept back the right side of a long black duster, hooking the fabric behind the holster from which protruded the butt of a pistol. A Colt .45 if Clare was not mistaken, and she wasn't. The Peacemaker, although it didn't look as if peace was the intent here.

"Eugene Doster." The name rolled out like an accusation.

It required a serious expenditure of self-control for Clare not to roll her eyes. She knew that voice.

The traveling salesman let out a squeak of terror and tried to scramble backward up the steps. Failing in this, he turned in a full circle, his eyes squeezed tight as his face passed Clare rapidly by.

"Here now, sir," the conductor said, reaching up a hand. He withdrew it when the voice spoke again. It had the quality of a large bronze bell, only hung at ground level instead at the top of the steeple, calling everyone to service, or in this case to attention, especially Mr. Doster.

With the sole exception, Clare noticed, of a man leaning against a wall, head back, eyes closed, and giving forth with an audible snore. He wore a hairy brown suit and a broad-brimmed hat the wall had pushed down over his eyes. His jacket, unbuttoned, slid open enough to reveal the silver star pinned to his waistcoat.

"Don't make me come up on that car after you, Eugene. My brothers and I did a job of work for the Santa Fe in Trinidad not long past. You were the foreman on that job and you skipped town without paying us the three hundred dollars you owed. I understand you're carrying the Santa Fe's payroll today. I'm not robbing you, I'm not even asking for interest, but you best pay up right quick or you won't make it from here to the dining room."

The sunlit path between the two men widened as the crowd drew back a little farther, just in case the man in the derby couldn't shoot straight. Clare wasn't worried. She'd seen him shoot before.

The locomotive exhaled in a puff of steam that was half chug, half scream. Everyone jumped, including the snoring man with the star pinned to his waistcoat, who dropped a nearly empty bottle when he jerked awake, smashing it into pieces on the platform and startling everyone all over again.

It was time to take remedial action. Clare let out a breathy little scream—nothing in comparison to Doster's, or the locomotive's for that matter—and managed to trip over her own feet in a move that would have done a Ringling Brothers Circus clown proud. She pitched headlong into Doster, arms flailing dramatically, carpet bag flying—it landed bottom down a few feet away—and they both fell forward into a heap at the foot of the stairs. The gallant conductor managed to catch Clare before she landed, using the opportunity to investigate all the portions of her anatomy he could reach before she struggled free.

"Oh my goodness!" She pulled on the hem of her jacket and he watched carefully as she pulled the fabric straight across her breast. So did every other man on the platform, excepting the man with the Peacemaker, who came forward in long strides. He grabbed Doster by the shoulders of his coat and hauled him to his feet. "Fork it over, Doster."

Doster fumbled with the twine holding his bag closed with shaking hands, finally getting it open enough to extract a fat envelope.

"That's the ticket," Peacemaker said approvingly. "Count it out. Three hundred. No more and no less."

Doster did, one bill at a time. Everyone watching counted along with him. Derby hat gathered up the bills, stuffed them inside his duster, and winked at Clare. "Welcome to Montaña Roja, ma'am."

Over his shoulder she saw the Montaña Roja Harvey House, which had a row of windows overlooking the train platform. Every window was crowded with women in the black dress and white bib apron of a Harvey Girl.

So she didn't dare do more than scoop up her bag and brush by Bat Masterson, Mr. Doster's debtor and one of the two other Pinkerton agents Robert Pinkerton had put on Fred Harvey's case. She did say, in as forceful a tone as one could muster in a whisper, "Behave."

She was just as certain that no one else heard her as she was that no one saw his hand pat her hip most unprofessionally as she passed him by.

The show over, the crowd dispersed. Clare made her way across the platform, passing the man wearing the star, who was beginning to slide down the wall.

"Hold up there, Uncle Fred," and Clare saw a second man catch him by one elbow and heave him back to the vertical, seemingly without effort. The second man was about the same height, with a muscular frame, the same lantern jaw, and this one had bright blue eyes. The man with the star still had his eyes closed. The second man winked at Clare and touched the brim of his hat. "How do, darlin'."

She inclined her head and went past them to the door into the restaurant. He leaped forward to open it for her, narrowly beating out a cowboy wearing a ten-gallon hat for the privilege. "Thank you, gentlemen."

And then the man who had winked at her had to turn fast to catch the man with the star before he fell face forward onto the platform.

## 5

"You're using muscles you didn't even know you had and they all hurt, and you feel as if you don't have time to breathe, never mind eat, sleep, or smile at the customers."

*Montaña Roja, New Mexico Territory*

### March, 1890

Clare distinctly remembered telling Fred Harvey that she didn't think she was suited to a life between four walls. That is, she remembered saying it when she had time for remembering anything other than keeping up with the tasks of her new job, which was not often during the next week. The very moment she stepped into the Montaña Roja Harvey House and identified herself to the manager she was told to don her uniform and get to work.

The manager, one Louis Abernathy, was a man of few words. In his mid-thirties, unmarried, he was of medium height and weight with an even-featured visage that might have been considered handsome but for the bold stare from unblinking dark eyes that seemed deliberately designed to instill discomfort in those he turned it on, particularly women.

He certainly subjected Clare to a free and full examination, head to toe, lingering where one might expect, but other than that treating her with a professional distance that felt almost unfriendly. She only wondered about that professional distance when she saw how familiarly he treated the other girls. Standing too closely one moment, a hand inappropriately placed at another, by the end of the first day she didn't wonder at the space most of the female staff took care to maintain between them when in conversation with the manager.

Chef was the god of the kitchen, a burly man in a double-breasted uniform that always began the day a spotless white and ended it looking as if he'd been cleaning out a cesspool. In all the time she spent at Montaña Roja she never learned his name; he was only ever Chef to all staff in both reference and address. When she was introduced he took one look at Clare and blushed deep red all the way up to his hairline, which action he repeated every single time he saw her thereafter. He never did manage to address her directly, although she heard him talking to others in the kitchen when she was out of his sight.

The other Harvey Girls were a blur of women in their late teens and early twenties, at first difficult to identify as individuals as they were constantly in motion. As a group they offered encouraging remarks, friendly instruction, and help when it was needed. During her first days help nearly always was needed if Clare was to avoid reprimand from the manager or the stewards.

Four of them stood out as individuals in her first days, in part because they worked the same shift. Florence Sellers was a fresh-faced farm girl from Kansas who looked as if she should still be in school. Henrietta Major, twenty and also from Kansas but from Kansas City, was less impressed with the glamor of waiting tables and seemed always to have one foot out the door. Ida Sterling was from Missouri, still in her teens and sending most of her salary home to support her parents, five brothers, and one sister because the family farm as run by her father could not. Elizabeth Higgins was from Nebraska and the eldest at twenty-five. Montaña Roja was her third Harvey House, after the one in Pueblo in Colorado and before that in Topeka. When there was a question about hours or wages or contracts, Elizabeth was the authority as well as their spokesman, and was by far and away the hardest and most capable worker of anyone on the staff.

Work Clare did, too, twelve hours a day, six days a week and sometimes seven. When she did have a day off it was given to washing and ironing her uniforms and, if she was lucky, catching up on her sleep. She had always considered herself to be in good physical condition but she woke her first morning with her body one giant ache. Her feet hurt, her back hurt, and her shoulders were so stiff she could barely turn her head to either side. Her hands were chapped and she said in an unguarded moment, "I had no idea this job would be so physically hard." She put a hand in the small of her back and stretched. It took an effort not to groan out loud. "You all make it look so easy." She watched Ida glide into the dining room, her back straight, her chin up, and her brow smooth, as if she was completely unaware of the tray on her shoulder laden with plates, bowls, cups, flatware, and napkins, the exact weight of which Clare was now all too familiar with. The monogrammed tableware was heavy enough for sea duty and much heavier full, especially when you were serving a table of eight with one eye on the clock and the other on the locomotive puffing a reminder of imminent departure outside.

"I remember—we all do!—our first days on the job." Florence's voice was kind as she moved around Clare to deal out plates like a sharp dealing out cards in a game he was making sure he would win. "You're using muscles you didn't even know you had and they all hurt, and you feel as if you don't have time to breathe, never mind eat, sleep, or smile at the customers. Don't worry, you'll soon grow accustomed."

Clare didn't doubt her but she did wonder where she would find the time to do her real job. Almost every passenger on every train passing through Montaña Roja opted for breakfast, lunch, or dinner, although families did occasionally gather on benches outside the windows to eat meals they had packed themselves. Those passengers who opted to eat inside must be served in thirty minutes, measured from the time the train arrived to the moment it left. It was only recently, Florence told her, that the House had begun to stay open all day to serve the general public of Montaña Roja. "The town doubled in size over the last six months, after the Argentine Mine discovery. You've heard of it?"

Clare had, a rich lode of silver halfway up the south face of one of the Sangre de Cristo Mountains. A narrow gauge railway had been constructed practically overnight to carry laden ore cars from the mine to the railhead north of town, and the men who were building both spur and mine flooded into the Harvey House whenever they managed to hit town. Most of them acted like seeing a Harvey Girl was the first time they'd ever seen a woman. It sometimes felt as if she was performing on a stage with every light focused directly on her, although she was kept far too busy, first learning her job and then doing it, to feel uncomfortable for long.

"Quickly, Clare, quickly, I can hear the train!"

The Harvey Houses reduced everything to the minimal amount of effort possible for the maximum result. Even the way the cups sat or didn't on their saucers was a signal from staff who took the orders to staff who brought the drinks. She ducked into the kitchen once to watch the cooks make every meal according to a preset menu that was repeated in every Harvey House kitchen every day without deviation. (Chef saw her, blushed, and tried to ladle soup with a spatula.) Supplies of fresh fruits and vegetables and dairy products and meat and seafood arrived daily in refrigerated cars.

"Clare! Take this meat loaf to the man at the counter before it gets cold!"

"Which man? They're all men."

"The one in the skimmer!"

Fred Harvey had told her that no refrigerated car had ever been stolen in any of the robberies, a fact she found worth noting. Was the intended destination of the stolen cars so distant that the contents of even a refrigerated car would spoil before they arrived? Was the distance between the place where the trains were robbed and their destination a criterion in stealing the stolen goods? Was it a criterion in finding them, or at least the cars they had been in when they were stolen?

"Clare! Table six needs a refill and more cream!"

When she wasn't taking orders, serving food or clearing up after a meal, she was making fresh coffee every two hours in huge silver urns. When she wasn't making coffee in the urns, she was polishing them. When she wasn't polishing the urns, she was polishing the silverware monogrammed with the Fred Harvey logo, an unending task.

"Clare! Can you get me another polishing cloth? This one is worn through."

Her first day when her shift was over she staggered upstairs and fell into bed and was instantly asleep.

She woke the next morning with the feeling that there was something she had missed the night before. The entirety of the small room was within sight without raising her head and she took her time examining every inch of it.

Her room had been searched.

The other girls shared two to a room; her room was the only single, situated near the back stair. She was certain this had been arranged but Abernathy, who as manager would be the obvious person through whom Harvey would choose her accommodations, had not by the lift of an eyebrow indicated any knowledge of her true identity or purpose. He certainly wasn't any easier on her than he was the other girls, as the ache in her lower back could attest.

Her room was small and narrow, with a nightstand, a two-drawer dresser sitting beneath a window, and a curtained alcove that served as the closet. The floor space was further cramped by a wooden chest sitting at the foot of the bed and the wooden rocking chair opposite it. It wasn't quite the luxuriously furnished bedroom with an adjacent private bathroom—here the bathroom was down the hall and communal—that she had enjoyed at the Calhouns' house in Bienville, Mississippi, but there were flush toilets and they were inside, a welcome surprise. The mattress and bedding were clean and comfortable and the door had a lock to which she had the key. She didn't know how many other keys might be in existence—that there must be at least one the search had made her aware—and so each night thereafter she took the added precaution of jamming a small chisel between the door trim and the wall, with the heavy wooden handle resting against the door. A well-placed kick would force entry but it would make enough noise to have her up and ready to meet the threat.

It was possible that she had read too many dime novels.

The intense fatigue brought on by a long journey and her first full day of work was probably why she hadn't noticed that the clothes in her closet were hanging in a different order than she had left them when she unpacked.

Well, well.

It could have been a petty thief, not unheard of in communal living. The entire staff, manager, chef, kitchen staff and Harvey Girls, lived above the kitchen and the restaurant.

Or, and what she found much more likely, the news that Fred Harvey had hired a Pink to find his stolen goods had leaked down the high iron from Kansas to the New Mexico Territory and someone concerned in the robberies wanted to find out how much she knew.

In which case they were disappointed. All she ever carried on the job that might give away her true identity was her notebook and derringer, and those items never left her. She had constructed the persona of Clare Wadsworth from the skin out specifically for this job and she was certain it would stand up to any scrutiny.

She left the closet as it was, and washed and dressed and reported downstairs for work. There was nothing in anyone's demeanor to indicate that they thought she was anything other than what she said she was, at least not yet.

The third night, a Friday, she was wakened by muffled giggling, followed by stealthy footsteps and the creak of the back door opening. She rose and peeped between the edge of the blind and the window. Henrietta, Florence, Ida, and Elizabeth along with two of the other Harvey Girls were climbing into the back of a wagon already occupied by a group of men she recognized as railroad workers. More giggling, immediately hushed, a light slap of leather on the backs of the horses and the wagon moved off, the wheels creaking even louder than the door had.

She slipped back beneath the covers and stared at the ceiling.

Fred Harvey had exacting standards for Harvey Girls' behavior and she had just witnessed a firing offense. Harvey Girls were mostly young, single women working away from home and parental supervision. This was a very new thing that already occasioned comment from society at large, much of it negative, much of it from women.

Probably mostly from married women who were jealous of the opportunities they'd missed themselves, she thought uncharitably.

Nevertheless, it was an unfortunate fact that Harvey Girls being "no better than they should be" was an opinion much shared. The men of the West held quite a different opinion, of course, but then they were also the ones sneaking the girls out at night. The Fred Harvey Company was determined to discourage any behavior that might reflect badly on either the company or their staff. Now that Clare had a front row seat, she suspected that the reasoning behind the rules had more to do with practicality than it did morality. Quite apart from the custom they brought into the Houses, especially in the woman-poor West, the Harvey Girls were just too important to the smooth running of the dining rooms, hence the strict rules that governed their behavior off the job.

She wondered if what she had just witnessed had had anything to do with her real job, and filed it away for future reference. After that she fell asleep, only to be woken again when the girls returned some hours later. The next day she endeared herself to all four of them (heavy-eyed and moving with less than the usual Harvey Girl celerity) by stepping up to help them complete their duties well and on time, thereby avoiding the attention of the manager.

One never knew where aid might come from when one needed it.

There were other restaurants in Montaña Roja but only one Harvey House. As the days passed she began to recognize repeat customers. Wash Gowan appeared to have appropriated the big round table in the southwest corner as his own. She was on the counter the first week and was not called on to wait on his table until her second. He was pleasant in manner but made no attempt at familiarity, for which she was grateful. It was more than she could say for too many of the other customers when she came out from behind the counter. The restaurant served liquor, with a list of mixed drinks on the menu, and no one, especially none of the guests at Gowan's table, left with less than two drinks under his belt. The stewards were always watching, though, and quick to intervene. Drunks were served but drunken behavior was not tolerated.

Gowan's guests were an interesting mix. He was often accompanied by the man who had kept the sheriff on his feet her first day in town. Gowan called him Bob. Bob called him Mr. Gowan. From the bits of conversation she overheard it sounded as if Bob ran Gowan's ranch.

One day they were joined by a tall, balding man with flourishing muttonchops who wore the uniform of the United States Cavalry and the insignia of a lieutenant colonel. The current commanding officer of Fort Union, she later learned, and noticed that Gowan summarily moved those already seated to place the colonel at his right hand. They had their heads together over most of the meal.

The sheriff was often present. He drank his lunch, beginning at the top of the drinks menu and working his way down to the bottom. It was a marvel to Clare that he never needed help getting to his feet or an escort out of the establishment. Or it could be that Gowan was one of the town's leading citizens and the sheriff wanted to keep his job and he knew enough about his own capacity to know when to stop.

Another regular guest was a thin, bent man with even less hair than the colonel, fingers that looked and moved like the legs of a white spider's, and an unbearably unctuous manner. Gowan never said a word that he didn't punctuate with a seated bow and a wheezing "Oh, yes, indeed, Mr. Gowan, I have often thought the same myself."

"Who is that dreadful creature?" she whispered to Florence in passing.

"Oh, him." Florence shuddered. "Uriah Heep to the life, isn't he?" She smiled when Clare smothered a laugh. "It's a wonder how Mr. Gowan can bear his company."

"Yes, but who is he?"

"Walter Dabney," Florence said over her shoulder on her way into the kitchen. "The Indian agent for the New Mexico Territory."

Which made Dabney the federal agent appointed to oversee relations with the Indian tribes, a position of tremendous power, as the agents were in authority over disbursement of federal funds to the reservations. A man with his fingers in as many pies as Gowan had would be willing to put up with any amount of obsequiousness to have first pick of supply contracts for such a vast market. Which was the only reason Clare could see for tolerating Dabney at table. It was taxing enough to wait on him, as he was wont to make fawning remarks about one's personal appearance in a manner as unwanted as it was offensive. Also, he spit as he spoke, spraying her and his dining partners on both sides with every word.

Another man, short, blessedly quiet, neat but never showy in his appearance, appeared more sporadically. Florence identified him as Dudley Platt, a local businessman (he was the principal owner of the Montaña Roja Trust and Savings Bank) and Montaña Roja's magistrate. "Although the rumor is that we'll have our own courthouse by next year, with our own judge."

As with the sheriff, Clare guessed that Gowan would have a great deal to say as to who that judge would be, which could explain Mr. Platt's joining Gowan for the occasional lunch.

The first day she waited on Gowan's table he paused while his guests left and murmured, "Very well done, Miss Wadsworth. No one would know this was your first House."

"Thank you, Mr. Gowan, you're very kind."

In clearing the table she discovered that he'd left a double eagle beneath his saucer. Florence nodded a little enviously when Clare displayed it. "Yes, he always leaves one of those. He's a lovely man, is Mr. Gowan. It's why we were all so jealous when Mr. Abernathy said you were to wait his table when he came in."

Clare looked up, startled, to meet Florence's inquisitive gaze. "What?"

"Oh, yes, that order came from the top. Mr. Gowan must have requested you. You came on the same train, didn't you?"

"Well, yes, but we barely spoke."

"Mmm." Florence nodded at the double eagle. "Put that away somewhere safe. It's his standard tip and everyone will know you have it."

Clare did better than that. The next day, between lunch and dinner service, she sought out the Montaña Roja Trust and Savings Bank and opened an account, and then she went back to the House and told everyone what she had done. Florence was impressed. "I never. Your own bank account?"

"Yes. You should open one, too." Clare looked around at the other girls, who were listening. "You all should."

"Yes, but banks fail, don't they?"

"Well, this one is in a very expensive, brand new building, so I expect they are solvent, at least for now." Clare shrugged. "And people who keep their money under their mattresses sometimes come home to find they have been robbed."

She had been reassured by Florence saying that the twenty-dollar gold coin bearing the proud, crowned head of Lady Liberty was Gowan's standard tip. She didn't want him singling her out in any way, at least not yet.

The last day of her first week in Montaña Roja she waited until the house was quiet and slipped downstairs to break into the manager's office. Bound ledgers and reports filled a shelf behind the desk. In one drawer she found a copy of every bill of lading going back to before construction had even begun on the Montaña Roja Harvey House. She was capable of reading a balance sheet (the bookkeeping course at Vassar had proved most useful in her chosen profession, if not quite in the way her teachers had envisioned) and with a swift scan of the numbers over time and factoring in other observations, she was able to draw some interesting preliminary conclusions.

Harvey would undoubtedly use another descriptor when he came to hear of them.

What most puzzled her was how easily those discrepancies were found.

A sound came from the kitchen, followed by a whisper. In one swift movement Clare snuffed the candle she had brought, shrouding it so there was no smell, replaced the ledgers and stepped swiftly and soundlessly to a door in the near wall, which she had opened when she came in. Inside was a closet with coat hooks and shelves and supplies and a broom and a bucket and a mop. She pulled the door almost closed behind her. Through the remaining crack she could see a corner of the desk, no more.

Two people, whispering. The light came on. There was a smothered giggle, the sound of the door closing, some fumbling. One voice, female, "Be careful! I don't own so many clothes I can afford to have you tear this skirt!"

Leather creaked, probably the brown chesterfield against the wall to the right of the door.

"Turn off the light." The woman again. Her voice sounded breathless, and also familiar.

"I want to see."

"I don't—oh!"

Clare really didn't want to have to listen to what was about to follow but shoving open the door to the closet and running out was not an option. She also really wanted to know who these two were on the off chance that this little encounter had anything to do with her investigation. All information was good information. She resigned herself and tried to focus on what was said and who might be saying it.

"Oh, what are you—Louis, what are you doing!"

His voice was muffled. "Hold your skirt out of the way."

"You've never done that b— Oh, oh… that feels, oh my, oh my goodness…"

Clare stared determinedly at the door and tried not to listen too closely to the activities on the other side of it. She was not ignorant of the ways men and women showed their affection, and not inexperienced, either, but it was so intensely private an activity that even just listening made her feel like a snoop of the worst kind.

"Ahhhhhhh, yes…" The woman half sobbed, half laughed, and then her voice trailed off on a long sigh.

There was the clink of a belt buckle and the rustle of clothing, followed by another "Oh!" from the woman. A rough thumping began, Clare assumed of the back of the chesterfield against the wall, along with the smack of flesh on flesh.

"Oh, yes, yes, yes, harder, oh…"

The thumping and the smacking speeded up and then stopped suddenly, followed by a deep, guttural groan.

For a few blessed moments all was still. Very carefully Clare pushed the closet door wide enough to see. A second only was needed to put names to the lovers. She pulled the door back to its previous position.

"Oh, my goodness, that was… that was…"

"You have to get back upstairs."

"I know, I know, but kiss me again." Soft sounds. "Mmmm. I can smell myself on you."

"You have to get back upstairs."

"No need to be in such a rush. Everyone's asleep."

"Let's make sure they stay that way. Come on."

"When can we meet again?"

"When I can. Get up."

"Louis? When?"

"Let's go."

The office door opened and closed and footsteps receded. There was the distant sound of creaking stairs.

Clare waited five excruciatingly long minutes to make sure they weren't in fact coming back for a second go before she emerged from the closet, and barely caught the broom before it crashed to the floor.

In the dim light the outlines of the House's ledgers were practically invisible on the shelves. She could have left them open on the desk. Abernathy and Henrietta would never have noticed.

The House manager and a Harvey Girl, engaged in unlawful sexual congress on the sofa in the House manager's office.

Definitely a firing offense, for both of them.

She sat down behind the desk again and relit her candle. There was notepaper in the center drawer and Abernathy had been so kind as to refill his fountain pen at the end of the day. She composed the letter in her head and translated it to Pitman on the page. When she was done she appropriated one of Abernathy's envelopes and addressed it to Mr. R. Smith at a mailbox in Chicago in the post office closest to the Pinkerton building.

The return address she left blank. She'd worked in small towns before.

## 6

"I'll die before I run!"
*Montaña Roja*

### March 26, 1890

#### Wednesday

The next day was her first split shift, which left her with six free hours before she had to begin setting up for the dinner service. She parried invitations from the other girls to join them in shopping expeditions or country walks and instead sallied forth on her own to find the post office and further explore the town. The quick trip to the bank having been her sole excursion to date, she was curious to see how the reality of the American West measured up to the adventures published by Messrs. Street & Smith.

What she found first and most surprising was the similarity between Montaña Roja and every other town the Atchison, Topeka and Santa Fe ran through: a grid of broad avenues with narrower streets crossing them perpendicularly, forming a perfect rectangle with the train station at its heart. A rectangle the same general shape as a railroad car, come to that. You could step down from any train on the high iron to any town it served and find your way around blindfolded.

Her first case had been the infiltration of a smuggling ring in Boston and she remembered without affection being too often lost in transit due to the city's fidelity to its pre-Revolutionary roots. Montaña Roja was infinitely easier to navigate.

The railroads were primarily in the business of transportation but it was no secret that the serious money was made in real estate. To encourage the building of trains the federal government had bestowed large tracts of land on the railroads on either side of the proposed routes, and the town grids were laid out to create lots for sale, all profits accruing to the railroads. From Kansas south and west, in every community the train had passed through, Clare had been deafened by the noise of hammers, saws, and the oaths of workmen as buildings went up in every direction.

That was no different here in the New Mexico Territory, either, where the vast quantities of sawdust in the air made her sneeze. The original town of Montaña Roja had been established by a land grant from the Mexican government and featured the traditional square plaza surrounded by the rest of the town. After 1848 and the Treaty of Guadalupe Hidalgo the trickle of American settlers down the Santa Fe Trail increased to a flood, followed hotfoot by the railroads. When the ATSF proposed to flatten the original town and replace it with their own, the inhabitants protested. In a hurry, as they always were, the ATSF solved the problem by moving the railhead a mile away, which inevitably placed the old town on the south side of the tracks and which now was where most of the Indians, Mexicans, and poor whites lived.

On the north side of the tracks, everything was so new it was almost painful to the eyes. The clock tower on the station building next door to the Harvey House was the highest structure in town. One street north was City Hall (next to the post office, where Clare bought a two-cent stamp and posted her letter), one corner down a bank (the Montaña Roja Trust and Savings Bank, owned by Mr. Gowan's friend Mr. Platt), turn another corner and find a library, walk to the northwest intersection of the last street (Tenth) with the last avenue (Tyler) and there was a school. It was no one-roomed clapboard schoolhouse but a long single-story building made of adobe bricks covered with plaster, with a baseball diamond out back, a pleasing mixture of old and new that was lacking anywhere else north of the tracks. There were plans for another, larger school already, she'd heard someone say over lunch.

There was a Protestant church with a tall steeple, but not so tall as the station clock tower. Both were dwarfed by the mountains behind them, as was everything else. The archbishop of Santa Fe had built a small but exquisite adobe church south of the tracks for the Hispanic citizens and the few Pueblo converts, where Padre Cristóbal presided. Clare had waited on him one day when he was meeting with his church elders over lunch, a balding, plump, cheerful man in a black cassock who wasn't horrified at being served by a woman. At least he didn't act like Clare was offering herself up for sale along with the meal the way the Reverend Junius Bean of the Fallen Angel Protestant Church of Red Mountain did.

A second theater was under construction, as the first was packed nightly to vaudeville acts and melodramas interspersed with the plays of Oscar Wilde, Henrik Ibsen, and the inevitable Shakespeare. Montaña Roja was still talking about the performance of *Macbeth* whose cast had mistaken some of their lines and had been encouraged by irritated audience members shouting out the correct ones. "But there was only a small riot," Florence said cheerfully, "and nobody died."

"This time," Ida said. "They should ban *Macbeth*. I don't see how a play about conspiracy, treason, and multiple murders can lead to anything but violence."

"Oh, you Puritan, you. Your parents aren't looking over your shoulder here, Ida. You can watch what you want without anyone threatening to send you straight to hell without your supper."

At first Clare thought that Ida might take offense, but then she relaxed and laughed. "I suppose. At any rate I haven't been led into a life of sin and perversion by any of the plays I've seen so far."

Florence laughed and hugged her.

There was a dance parlor with a house band open every night of the week including Sundays, and an opera house was set to open in May with a grand performance by Adelina Patti reprising her signature role as Zerlina in *Don Giovanni*. It was said that the ATSF was laying on a special car just for Madame Patti and her entourage. Clare did not care for opera (she had attended a few in Chicago and found it to be too much like being shouted at at full volume nonstop for three hours) but were she still in Montaña Roja when

Madame Patti performed, she would definitely plunk down her money for a ticket, if only to watch the audience reaction.

The town's population was, to put it mildly, diverse. On a single one-way stroll down Washington Avenue, one encountered Mexicans in dusty sombreros and Indians in Levi's and tanned leather tunics and Chinamen with baggy cotton trousers and black braids down to their waists. There were businessmen in suits, cowboys in chaps, miners in Levi's, and farmers in overalls. There was a large number of black people, mostly men but some women with children, too, all of whom took care to avoid cowboys. Many cowboys were Texans. For them the Civil War was not over and they enjoyed taking their wounded feelings out on any available target, with slaves freed by the Emancipation Proclamation always their first choice. Clare saw more than one shoved into the street by some chaps-wearing yahoo who didn't think the other man should be walking on the same boardwalk he was.

Surprisingly, she saw black men in cowboy attire, too, and wondered how they were treated by their fellows on ranches and trail drives. It could not possibly have been a pleasant experience. On the other hand, the Pinkertons had their ear to the ground all over the nation and some of the reports from the Southern states recounting ongoing racial attacks were hard to read. In Bienville she had only seen the Calhouns interacting with their cook and maid, and if there was little respect—on either side—she hadn't seen any outright abuse. Of course Mary Calhoun would never have behaved in such a manner before a guest she believed to be the kind of lady to which she herself aspired.

There was at least one saloon per block, which accounted for the state of public drunkenness everywhere in evidence. Clare herself quickly learned to step into the hard-packed dirt of the street to avoid colliding with men lurching through screen doors voluntarily or with assistance. Of course the street provided its own challenges in the way of horses and wagons and, once, if her eyes did not deceive her, a chariot? She'd never seen one outside of a history book so she couldn't be sure. The woman driving it was dressed in blue velvet trimmed in black satin that exactly matched the coats of the chariot's two gleaming black horses. The three of them appeared supremely indifferent to the attention they were receiving from all sides. Clare thought the driver might be someone worth knowing but the chariot vanished into the crowd and Clare never saw it or her again. She would come to find that that happened often in Montaña Roja.

So did gunfights. Almost every man she saw wore a revolver in a holster belted low. Since most of them were also drunk it required very little in the way of provocation to pick a fight. That first day Clare saw two men trying desperately to hit each other stumble out of a saloon off the boardwalk and into the street. One of them was laughing uncontrollably and dropped prone into the dirt, where he hooted loudly enough to frighten the mourning doves perched on the false fronts of the buildings. The other man was not laughing and grabbed at his revolver but was too drunk to find the butt. The crowd fled for the sides of the street, Clare not excluded.

The first man staggered to his feet, still laughing, and managed to choke out, "Aw, c'mon, Johnny! It was only a joke!"

Johnny kept pawing unsuccessfully at his holster. "Run, Georgie, you sumbitch! Run before I give you a new hole to drain out all a your bullshit!"

The laughing man stopped laughing. "Run, my ass, Johnny O'Leary, I'll die before I run!"

Johnny finally got his gun out but by then Georgie had leveled his. There was a boom! followed a moment later by a second boom! Both men were momentarily obscured in a drift of gun smoke. No one moved until the smoke cleared, revealing Georgie staring at Johnny on the ground. Georgie's shot had caught him in the gut. He was clutching at it with blood-covered hands, screaming.

His own shot had gone wide. A general store's large picture window now lay in shards on the boardwalk.

After what felt far too long but was in truth only moments, Johnny stopped screaming. His last breath was half gargle, half snarl. His hands relaxed and fell to his sides, revealing the ghastly, gaping wound of torn flesh and intestines. He stared unblinking up at the sky. In death he didn't look old enough to vote. He probably wasn't.

A woman screamed. Other than that there was little reaction from the crowd. A few men looked sick; a few women had handkerchiefs pressed to their mouths. No one fainted. After a moment a short cowboy whose spurs jingled cheerfully strode forward, pulled the red bandana from around his neck and spread it over Johnny's face. Clare appreciated the sentiment but thought over the wound would have been a better use of the bandana.

Georgie stood for a moment, weaving. "Oh, hell. He was a good partner. But he never could hold his liquor." And he stumbled up onto the boardwalk and back into the saloon. No one moved to stop him.

Clare drew a shaken breath. That certainly wasn't something you'd see on Michigan Avenue in Chicago, but judging by the demeanor of the onlookers in Montaña Roja it was just another Wednesday.

The saloon doors swinging behind the killer seemed to be the signal for the crowd to come back to life. Oxen pulling wagons, a black man pulling a cart laden with dry and canned goods and farm tools, vaqueros in silver-trimmed chaps on horseback, all stepped carefully around the body. In some distant part of her mind Clare thought someone surely ought to fetch the sheriff.

She looked up and across the street saw Gowan's foreman. Or no, this man wore a silver star on his waistcoat. He stood leaning against the wall of the Montaña Roja Trust and Savings Bank, his arms crossed as they had been on the platform that day, his short-crowned hat tipped down so that the narrow brim hid his eyes.

Perhaps an undertaker, then. There must be at least one in Montaña Roja or the town would be unlivable.

The indifferent manner on display by the majority of the town's population made her feel as if she had hallucinated the whole incident, the fight, the death. The body itself would vanish in the next moment, leaving only a thin trail of blood in the hard-packed dirt of the street.

She looked around again for just one person who, like her, could still see the body, the awkward, sprawling remains of a young man who had melted out of existence only moments before. Surely it was only moments before?

Her gaze was caught by a tall, very thin man in his early thirties and balding, with deep-set dark eyes. He stood on the boardwalk in front of the shattered window, dressed in a faded blue button-down shirt and Levi's cuffed over high-heeled boots. He held a hat that looked older than he was at his side. He nodded once, pulled his hat on, and walked away.

There was a blast of hot alcohol-laden breath on her cheek and she jumped, her heart thudding in her ears. A young man in the uniform of a cavalry trooper. "Never mine, little lady. Happenzalla time. Nothing to bother your putty head about." He frowned, thinking, and then his expression cleared. "Pretty. Pretty head." He hiccuped. "Buy you a drink?"

Oddly, soldiers in uniform were the only men she saw unarmed. She inquired later and was told that most of the soldiers seen in town were on leave from Fort Union and were required to deposit their weapons at the post armory before being allowed out of the gate. They patronized the saloons every bit as much as any other man and they were subsequently as prone to inebriation and fighting, but none of them died.

The Harvey House was on their leave itineraries, too. He blinked at her. "Shay, dint you sherve me my lunsh yesterday? Besht bizkits ever I et!"

She was about to excuse herself when a hand slid into the crook of her elbow. "I'm sorry, sweetheart, I didn't mean to keep you waiting so long," and she looked around to see Bat Masterson standing next to her. He tipped his bowler to the young soldier. "Thank you for looking after my wife, good sir," and guided her down the sidewalk and around the corner.

As soon as they were out of sight she halted, freeing her arm. "Hello, Bartholomew."

He shook his head and propelled her down the street and into a small coffeehouse, where he seated them at a secluded corner table—appropriating, as always, the seat that put his back to the wall—before turning his considerable charm on their waitress. She was a pretty girl barely into her teens, who listened breathlessly to his order and proceeded to serve them what looked like everything in the kitchen.

He removed his bowler and set it carefully to one side, smoothed the hat line out of his dark hair, and turned his best smile Clare's way. It was a good smile, even she had to admit that, full of white, even teeth, and their waitress certainly agreed when she came to refill the cups they had barely sipped from. "How have you been, sweetheart?"

His eyes were a lovely velvety brown, with thick lashes the envy of any girl who looked upon them. Clare looked around to see if anyone was within earshot. "That's Miss Wadsworth to you. Bartholomew."

"It's Bat, sweetheart, as you well know, and everyone here knows."

She tried not to grit her teeth. He called her "sweetheart" because he knew it annoyed her and the only way to get him to stop was to ignore it. "All the more reason we shouldn't be seen speaking in public."

He leaned toward her and quirked his eyebrows. "Why, Miss Wadsworth, had I only known, I would have gotten us a room." He laughed at her expression. "How'd the trip go?"

"It went fine until it almost didn't when you just had to brace that fellow on the train."

"He owed me money, sweetheart, what can I say?" His expression hardened momentarily, the gun for hire showing through the elegant exterior. "Couldn't let that stand, now, could I?"

"Evidently not."

The charmer returned with an easy grin at her tart reply.

Clare had worked a case with Bartholomew "Bat" Masterson in Chicago. They had played a couple, a role Bat had entered into with a little too much enthusiasm. He'd taken her rejection in good part, however, and when the case concluded went off to be the sheriff in Trinidad, Colorado. "What happened to the sheriff's job?"

He shrugged. "The railroad got built, the town settled down, job got boring. I was fine with moving on when the Pinks asked." He quirked an eyebrow. "Saw Wash Gowan get off your train. You manage to meet him?"

"I did."

"And?"

She raised her shoulders in a slight shrug. "He nibbled at the hook."

"Poor bastard." He sampled an iced cake. "Not bad. Not the Polish Bakery in Chicago, but then what is?" He washed it down with a swallow of coffee. "Also not bad. Love mining towns for that reason alone, they always import the best in their efforts to separate miners from their money." He licked his fingers and then wiped them fastidiously on a napkin. He leaned forward and dropped his voice to a level only she could hear. "All right. I got here before you so I took the time to do a little nosing around, in both what passes for high society in Montaña Roja, and low." His smile was smug. "People talk to me, you know."

She knew. It was, admittedly, in part due to his charm of manner, which was considerable. But it had much more to do with people wanting to trade what might be their only currency—information—to pay for time spent in the company of a man of Bat Masterson's reputation. "And?"

"There are a lot of rumors about the train robberies, Clare, but most of them I'd classify as just that: rumors. Whoever is doing this has managed to keep a lid on it. Hell, half the town's population is drunk a hundred percent of the time and even when they're sobbing their hearts out all over your best suit they've got nothing interesting to say. I have managed to ferret out a little background on the town's leading citizens."

She raised her eyebrows invitingly.

He chuckled. "All right. Let's start with George Washington Gowan. He's from back east, West Virginia, son of a coal miner, worked his way up in the mine's organization from the pits to the office. By eighteen he was managing. By twenty he owned it." He contemplated the plate of pastries and chose a tiny cake with half a strawberry on it. He picked off the strawberry and ate it and put the cake back.

"The local miners, he's a huge favorite of theirs. The coal miner who made it rich. They talk about him all the time, but never anything to do with what we're interested in. Anyway, that mine back in West Virginia was the bottom rung of the ladder that led him up into the rarefied air breathed only by such luminaries as Astor and Morgan and

Rockefeller and Carnegie. By my reckoning he owns about a half of the New Mexico Territory by now."

"Half?"

"Well, maybe only a quarter." He examined the pastry plate again, and this time selected a bite-sized caramel bar. It disappeared. Back to the pastries. A tiny praline. Crunch.

"He's stepped on a lot of toes on the way up, although that just seems to give the miners more call to admire him. They say Gowan forced out his first partner for pennies on the dollar. They say he personally caused the failure of a New York bank when they annoyed him with too high an interest rate." He wagged his finger. "One rumor I was able to track down to its source because the man still lives in the Territory, although in Santa Fe, which is a long and dusty ride from here."

"I'm sure you weren't thirsty for long after you got there. Put it on your expense sheet."

"You know I will."

"What did the man in Santa Fe have to say?"

"His name is Chester Weibert, known familiarly as Chessie. He's a dried-up, bitter old coot who has absolutely nothing nice to say about Gowan."

"Why is that?"

"Chessie says Gowan was in it with a fellow named Walter Dabney. He's—"

"The local Indian agent. I've waited on him at Gowan's table." She shuddered, a not entirely affected reaction.

"I've not seen him yet but Chessie says you can smell him coming."

"What did they do?"

"Again, according to Chessie, Gowan stole cattle and sold them to Chessie for next to nothing. Chessie sold them to Dabney and Chessie says Dabney inflated the average weight of the beeves when he bought them for the Indians. Somebody must have checked and it came back at him and he was fined. So then he was underwater on his ranch. He got a loan from the local bank—"

"Dudley Platt. Also the magistrate."

He nodded. "Chessie says Platt told him he had to put a high interest rate on the loan because of the federal government's disbarring Chessie from doing business with them for three years."

"So of course he couldn't make the payments."

"Not hardly. He was forced to sell, and guess who bought it?"

"Gowan."

"Give the little lady a prize."

She couldn't take much credit. None of this was in any way uncommon in what Mark Twain had dubbed the Gilded Age.

A movement caught the corner of her eye and she turned to see Elizabeth Higgins walking past the window at a brisk pace, several packages wrapped in brown paper and tied with string in her arms. She hoped the other girl hadn't seen her, or who she was with. Bat Masterson was a little too well known for her taste.

She looked back at Bat to see him regarding her with a raised eyebrow. "Just what am I doing here, Clare? Other than tracking down information for you, which I'm happy to do, but it doesn't really make best use of my talents." He inspected the pastry plate. "Yet."

She cocked an eyebrow right back. "I was hoping you could tell me. So far as I can see this is a straightforward theft investigation. A big one, and multiple thefts, true, but still."

He stroked his neatly clipped mustache meditatively. "I like the sound of that. Spells bonus."

"It does, but..."

"What?"

"Did he really send Tom down here, too?"

"Tom? Tom Horn?"

She nodded.

"Jesus Christ." His lips pursed in a silent whistle. "What're the B's expecting, another Lincoln County War?"

Thoughts of that bloody conflict pleased neither of them. Billy the Kid had been dead almost nine years but plenty of other gunfighters had stepped up to fill his shoes. They were employed by men who had followed Horace Greeley's admonition to go west and, if not grow up with the country, then to acquire as much of it as they could as fast as possible. A lot of them had taken that literally, usually at the point of as many guns as they could hire.

"You're sure they sent him along, too? Maybe Bob was just joshing you."

"I saw him. Today."

"Tom?"

"Yes. He was across the street from the shooting. He nodded at me and walked off."

"Great." Bat drank coffee. "And why us at all, anyway? No question local law enforcement is under strength and mostly drunk on the job, but the Army's only one stop up the tracks. Why not pull some strings in D.C. and send in the cavalry?" He snorted. "Better by far than a loose cannon like Tom."

"Do you know anything about Tom Horn?" She did. She'd worked with him before, too.

"Other than that he hits what he aims at? No."

"He hasn't had it easy."

Masterson snorted. "Who has?"

Nettled, she said, "He had a ranch in Arizona that was raided by rustlers. It bankrupted him and he lost the ranch. That was when he went to work as a range detective. It's personal for him."

"It's personal for all of us, sweetheart."

She gave him a long, thoughtful look.

"What?" He picked up one of the little cakes and ate it whole.

"Would you have shot him?"

"Who?"

"The man at the station that day. The one who owed you $300."

It took him a moment to remember. "Oh. Him." He shrugged. "Didn't have to, did I?"

They sat in silence until their waitress returned with more coffee. Masterson waved her off with a smile that sent her back to the kitchen with her shoes two feet above the floor. "Well, you did come bearing news, sweetheart, I'll say that for you. I better stock up on ammunition."

She thought it might be a good idea if she did, too.

"I'll stop in at the Harvey House most days. Give me the high sign if you need me. If you need me before that, I'll be at the Plaza." He smirked. "And if I'm not there, some saloon or other."

"Remember the bonus, Bat."

He picked up his derby and tapped it into place on his head. "I never forget a bonus, sweetheart. Don't worry, I'll be there when I'm needed."

He left. She waited for five minutes before following him.

She spent the rest of the afternoon completing her tour of the town through the mercantile district. On either side of and across from City Hall, a row of stores and shops with large windows contained displays of the goods off the most recent train. One of the displays featured a woman's green-and-blue plaid dress with long puffed sleeves and a row of pearl buttons running from neck to hem, accompanied by a straw hat with matching trim. As Clare watched, a clerk removed the dress and hat from the dummy and ten minutes later a woman walked out of the store's front door wearing it, trying hard to appear unconscious of the admiring and on occasion frankly lascivious stares of every passing male, although a tiny smile gave her away.

During the previous evening's dinner service Clare had waited on a woman wearing a satin Worth mantle that would not have looked out of place at Delmonico's in New York City. Her husband wore the latest style of homburg and a tailored three-piece suit with the obligatory gold watch chain ending in a fob made in the shape of a gold pan. It wasn't quite large enough to be vulgar but it made a statement. They both looked as if they had been outfitted from this same store.

Much of the money earned extracting silver ore from the Argentine was being as skillfully extracted by stores selling luxury goods on the avenues of Montaña Roja. She wondered briefly if she might be in the wrong business.

Of course she had also served women in riding trousers and even in Levi's and everything in between. Everyone came to eat at Fred's because it was the best meal between there and Chicago. Or between there and the Harvey House in Trinidad, where they could have eaten the exact same dinner that was being served in Montaña Roja. It was a truly Herculean task of planning and logistics that could never have been dreamed of before the iron horse superseded the four-legged one, and her hat was off to the man who had come up with the idea and then had convinced the Santa Fe Railroad it was a good one.

As it had proved in a remarkably short time.

And, alas, as with any organization run by human beings, it was subject to waste, fraud, and abuse on a scale befitting the chain's reach. In the New Mexico Territory there were already a dozen Harvey Eating Houses, and the staff in Montaña Roja was all agog at the recent news that Fred was building a hotel on the last avenue, which was halfway up the side of the first of the foothills, guaranteeing a sweeping view of the town and the high desert beyond. It was a topic of much discussion between servings. It was understood to be not a place for train passengers per se but more for rich Easterners and Europeans traveling in the American West just to look around.

"Like that Grand Tour the English take in Europe?" Henrietta said, fascinated.

Chef nodded, every inch the authority on foreign travel even though he'd never been east of the Mississippi River. So long as he didn't look directly at Clare, or have to speak in simple declarative sentences longer than five words.

"But there's nothing here like there, is there," Florence said. "No big old cathedrals or museums or castles. Or even cities."

"There is scenery," Ida said hesitantly. "What about that big canyon that is supposed to be west of here? In the Arizona Territory?"

One of the stewards shrugged. "Who's going to pay good money to look at a ditch in the ground?"

"People with more money than brains," the other steward said. "Plenty of those around."

A voice said mildly, "Who's going to pay good money for a crew to stand idle, flapping their gums instead of doing their jobs?"

Abernathy stood watching them scuttle off, Clare included, with no display of either disapproval or of satisfaction. A difficult man to read. Catching Henrietta's baffled expression in an unguarded moment, Clare thought she was not the only person to think so.

A week later, as she and Florence stood side by side, polishing serving spoons, Florence took a quick look around and said in a voice barely above a whisper, "Tornado."

"What?" Clare had experienced a tornado on the job in the Midwest and she did not care to experience another. She stood on tiptoe and craned her neck to see out the window. "It's clear out, no clouds. And I never heard tornados were common in this part of the country."

Florence chuckled. "This one is."

The following day the tornado arrived in the form of Fred Harvey himself on the noon train. Between breakfast and lunch that morning there had been an air of suppressed excitement among the staff, mixed in with some trepidation and, if Clare was not mistaken, a soupçon of terror. Abernathy was brusque and snappish, Chef more than ordinarily monosyllabic, and the stewards positively hunted each of the girls as they went about their work. Elizabeth had to reset one of her tables twice, and Clare was ordered to replace the tablecloth on hers because of a stain invisible to her eyes.

No one, Clare noticed, seemed particularly upset by their superiors' behavior. Indeed, they took every opportunity to watch for the arrival of the train through the window. At the first blast of the whistle someone shouted from the kitchen, "Here he comes! Let's do him proud!"

Clare just so happened to be standing next to a window with a clear view of the incoming train and so was perfectly positioned to watch Fred Harvey hop down from the engine to the platform carrying a valise. He tossed a salute to the engineer and made for the restaurant at a brisk trot, blowing through the door like a stiff breeze.

Clare noticed that everyone did their best to look surprised.

He greeted Abernathy briefly and commenced a thorough tour, beginning with the U-shaped counter that encircled the two enormous silver coffee urns on their pedestals, followed by every single table surrounding it and ending with every stovetop, oven, sink, counter, and shelf of the kitchen. Fortunately, the dining room passed muster, causing a not entirely silent exhalation of relief among the

Girls. Alas, the kitchen staff was not so fortunate. After one sip Fred condemned the albondigas soup as having been made with butter. Fred himself picked up the soup pot and poured it out the back door, and Chef stood threateningly over the dishwasher as he scoured the pot and then hovered over the trembling undercook, who started a new batch of onions in a rapidly melting lump of lard.

Other than Chef's red face the kitchen crew took this draconian action without flinching, and when Fred paused in following Mr. Abernathy into his office, "Travel—" the entire staff roared the words with him "—follows good food routes!" He laughed and waved and disappeared behind the office door.

All this Clare caught in glimpses as she took orders, coded the cups, served drinks and food, cleaned up spills, cleared plates, made coffee, and polished silver. Not by the quiver of an eyelid had Fred Harvey betrayed that he knew her, or that he had felt the twist of paper she had slid into his waistcoat pocket when she brought coffee and sandwiches into the office.

That day her shift ended at mid-afternoon. She retired to her room and stripped out of her uniform and hung it carefully behind the curtain, after which she washed up and went to bed and immediately to sleep. She woke again at precisely fifteen minutes before nine that evening.

She went down the hall to the lavatory for a quick wash, hearing voices and muted laughter behind the doors. Back in her room she brushed out her hair before putting it up into a Gibson girl updo, a less severe style than was required of a Harvey Girl, which style was primarily to keep their hair out of the food. She shook out her best shirt and put it on, carefully doing up the tiny mother-of-pearl buttons. There was a positive froth of lace at the throat and wrists instead of just a single thin line, much less severe and much more feminine than her everyday shirts. She donned skirt and jacket and pulled the lace cuffs free of the sleeves of her jacket and buttoned it up to just below the froth of lace. The white plume on her cap was loose. A few quick stitches put it right.

She pinned it on her hair, pulled on her gloves, and she was ready. When she heard the footsteps in the hallway, she opened her door a crack. "Mind if I join you?"

They all jumped.

She batted her eyes. "Please?"

Florence muffled a laugh. "We thought you'd never ask! But how did you know we were going out tonight?"

Clare did her best to look guilty. "I'm afraid I overheard Ida and Elizabeth talking about it this morning. Forgive me."

Henrietta made a face. "Quiet, before we wake the whole house! Come on, then, if you're coming!"

Clare slipped into the hallway, closed and locked her door behind her, and followed them out the door and down the stairs to the wagon that was waiting by the side of the avenue, at a distance carefully calculated by its cowboy driver to be just beyond earshot of the house.

## 7

Her third partner was the young cowboy she had watched kill his friend in the street.

### April 3, 1890

### Thursday

They drove straight to the Lightfoot Music and Dance Parlor, where the band played the oldest tunes in rotation with the latest tunes on strings and brass, and often everyone sang along. It was a pleasant place, with a high ceiling and benches alternating with tables and chairs against the walls, the band set up on a small stage at the back of the room, and a smooth wooden floor polished to a high shine. A station near the door collected everyone's sidearms, of which there was a fierce pile overflowing the compartments of a large cabinet set against the wall. The weight of her derringer felt particularly heavy in the hidden pocket of her skirt as she walked past, and she couldn't help but notice that no one was suggesting the men leave their knives behind. Every other man present wore one in a belt sheath, everything from jackknifes to skinning knives to old-fashioned Bowie knives. The latter looked capable of taking out more people faster than a six-shooter.

A pleasant matron standing behind a lectern accepted the entrance fee of one whole dollar, which seemed to Clare an extortionate amount. Dance parlors in Chicago charged five cents.

"Oh," she said, "I didn't know about the entrance fee—"

"No charge for women," Florence said. "Only the men pay."

Looking around the room she saw that the men outnumbered the women by ten to one. This would have given her cause for concern except that the men all seemed relatively sober, an uncommon sight in public in Montaña Roja. A third station served soft drinks and snacks. "No liquor?"

Florence shook her head firmly. "Only soft drinks, and anyone who goes outside to drink and tries to come back in is asked to leave. Oh," she said at Clare's look, "they try it on, of course. But none of us will dance with them if we smell liquor on their breath, and they know it. What they think is even worse is that if we turn them in for drinking, they're banned for a month." She nodded at the matron behind the lectern, who, now that Clare thought of it, had a very firm chin. "Mrs. Billingsley is the wife of the proprietor, and she has a knack for remembering faces. No one gets by her if she says they don't."

There was no one standing next to or behind Mrs. Billingsley. "Who enforces her commands?"

Florence laughed. "You make her sound like a general." She nodded at the crowd of men, who seemed to be standing nearer the door since the Harvey Girls came in. "They do. They enjoy coming here and they don't want to lose the privilege. They police themselves."

The cowboy of the jingling spurs, wearing a brand new red bandana tied around his neck, came up to sweep Florence out on the floor for a waltz. Clare was claimed by a whiskery young miner who was an unexpectedly good dancer; he told her he was from New York originally, come west to make his fortune and redeem himself in the eyes of a family who had cast him off when he flunked out of his fifth college. When the music stopped her hand was claimed by a bank clerk, who told her in all earnestness that she was the prettiest girl in Montaña Roja and how did she feel about marriage? Which made her wonder how accurate Florence was about the no liquor rule. But it turned out that he was perfectly sober and perfectly in earnest. She let him down as gently as she could and later that evening he polkaed past with Ida, and Clare heard him say, "You're the prettiest girl in Montaña Roja, ma'am." Over his shoulder Ida rolled her eyes at Clare.

Every level of Montaña Roja society appeared to patronize the Lightfoot Music and Dance Parlor. Clare saw husbands with women who were obviously their wives and other men dancing with women who obviously weren't. Older couples moved across the floor in stately fashion, young ones galloped through the steps, middle-aged ones escaped parenthood for a few precious hours to remember what each other looked like. Everyone was having a marvelous time and she'd heard much worse bands in Chicago. And against every square foot of wall leaned the shoulders of a cowboy or a miner or a sheepherder on the alert for the end of a song and his chance to have a woman in his arms for a few precious moments.

Her third partner was Georgie, the young cowboy she had watched kill his friend in the street. Tonight his clothes were neat and clean, his hair was combed, and his eyes were clear and steady and hopeful as he held out his hand, which had no blood on it. "If you please, miss—?"

Casting a swift look around, Clare saw no one staring in horror, and perforce accepted the killer's hand and allowed herself to be led out onto the floor. The band was playing a Strauss waltz, the "Blue Danube" if she was not mistaken, and the grace and melody of the music only added to the unreality of the situation. The killer, who introduced himself as George Quinn, was thrilled at the honor of dancing with a Harvey Girl. She knew this because he told her so, three or four times.

She had never danced with A.J. Calhoun, who was the last murderer she'd had anything to do with.

Georgie asked for the next dance and she refused with a smile that visibly took the sting out of her rejection, after which she sought out Florence, who was perspiring. All the Harvey Girls were having their feet danced off their ankles and the band showed no signs of stopping. "Florence, is there a—"

"Yes, of course! Indoors, too!"

Clare followed Florence's pointing finger to a narrow hallway that led behind the stage.

There was also a back door and no one to see as she slipped outside.

The night was cold and she walked quickly out to the street to see Fred Harvey waiting next to a buggy with a horse standing patiently between the shafts.

He handed her in wordlessly and shook the reins. The horse stepped forward obediently.

"Back to my hotel?" Harvey said softly.

As softly she replied, "Too risky. We might be seen and I can't imagine that that would help the investigation. Could we perhaps just drive?"

"Certainly. Here." He handed her a thick lap robe and she spread it over her legs, grateful for its warmth. "In fact, I'll take you to one of my favorite views. It should be deserted at this time of night."

He kept to the narrower and less populated streets, leaving the avenues to the roisterers who ruled supreme in the evening hours. There was the occasional gunshot but none so near that Clare felt the need to duck.

"Are there no liquor laws at all in Montaña Roja?"

She felt more than saw him shake his head. "The town is too new, with too many young men making too much money spending it all too quickly."

And too many with an interest in helping them spend that money, she thought, which they would no doubt be even happier to spend drunk. "What happens when the silver runs out and the timber is all cut down and the cattle eat all the grass?"

"Good question, given the ghost towns that are already beginning to litter the west. Western Colorado…" He shook his head and sighed. "But if I had to guess, I'd say that Montaña Roja is one of the towns that will survive. They're on the high iron, there are many and diverse business interests, they have a large labor force that increases with the arrival of every train, they have enough community spirit to build schools and government buildings and install the new incandescent bulb street lights, and best of all they have good and plentiful water in the Rio Rojo. So long as it snows every winter, they'll never run out, which is more than you can say for many of the newer communities." He shrugged. "They're low in skilled workers, true, but that's a common problem in every American community from the Atlantic to the Pacific."

"A few days ago I saw a man shot down in the street. There must have been a hundred people watching. No one tried to stop it. The sheriff was there and he did nothing. The man who killed him walked back into the saloon. And I just danced with him. To a Strauss waltz."

"Yes." He sounded philosophical. "Law enforcement is also a problem. There is a sheriff, as you say, but…" Harvey cleared his throat. "Which is why I sought recourse to Pinkerton's, and to you, Miss Wright."

They had left the road behind and were driving through stiff grass that crackled beneath the wheels. They came to the top of a small rise and Harvey turned the horse so that they overlooked the town. They sat quietly for a few moments, taking in the view.

As her eyes adjusted to the darkness, she saw piles of lumber and loose stones and bags of concrete and wooden crates. "Is this where you will build your new hotel?"

"Where did you hear about that, Miss Wright?"

"It's all anyone can talk about at the House. Face it, Mr. Harvey. Everything you do is news."

"I see. Yes, this is the front of the site. We'll start building as soon as the men and all the materials arrive."

Clare faced forward again and sighed. "I should think people will stand in line to rent a room with this view."

The knoll they were sitting on was above and behind the town, which made it one of the first foothills rising to the mountains behind. The high flat desert rolled out beneath a black sky sewn with clear crystals that shivered in their own reflected light. She recognized some of the constellations—her education had been a good one—Ursas Major and Minor, Cassiopeia perched tentatively on the horizon. Orion was either already down or not yet up, the same with the Pleiades. The half moon had set hours before but Clare didn't miss it. She let out a long, shaky sigh. "I've never seen anything like this. It is the most extraordinarily beautiful country."

She felt him look at her. "You think so?"

"I think I fell in love with it the moment we came down out of the Rocky Mountains." A little embarrassed by her own fervor she said abruptly, "I don't have a great deal to report, Mr. Harvey, but I have discovered a few things."

"Excellent. Let's hear them."

"First of all, you need better locks on your office doors."

"I beg your pardon?"

"I was able to pick the one on the manager's office in thirty seconds," she said absently, attention still fixed on the magnificence of the night sky, "and I am not a professional lockpick by any means. Although I warn you that the professional who tutored me in that fine art could have opened the safe you have in there in five minutes or less."

"I see." There was a faint quiver in his voice and she warmed to the man. It was so much easier working for someone who had a sense of humor. It was a quality totally lacking in the B's. Although that might have more to do with who she was than with their character.

"One thing I am curious about."

"What's that?"

"Fred Harvey Houses has the Girls sign contracts promising they won't marry for at least their first six months on the job, and you see to it that we share living quarters with the manager and the stewards, who I assume are tasked with chaperoning us. You recruit farm girls of good family—you even required letters from their ministers!—and you're concerned enough about the reputation women have when they work away from home that you've put these rules in place to convince the general population that we aren't all floozies."

"Floozies," he said, again with that slight tremor. "No indeed. And?"

"And I'm sitting here with you this evening because half your staff snuck out of the house to go dancing."

"So you are, and so they did." This time he allowed himself a brief chuckle. "The Girls work hard, Miss Wright. By now you yourself know how hard. Everyone who works hard needs to blow off a little steam now and then. Who am I to tell them they can't? The Lightfoot seems like a perfectly respectable place, regulated as to firearms and alcohol by its owners, patronized by citizens high and low in Montaña Roja. And the Girls are going and coming as a group, which means they're reasonably safe until they're tucked up securely in bed once again."

He sighed. "And they are girls, Miss Wright. Young girls, most of them, the majority of whom have spent their lives miles from the nearest town. Work as a Harvey Girl is excitement, adventure, travel, and, yes, romance. Many of them marry employees of the Santa Fe, which keeps Santa Fe management happy, too."

She could think of one Harvey Girl who thought she was going to marry into Fred Harvey middle management. She had not told him of the scene she'd witnessed in Abernathy's office between the manager and Henrietta Major, and unless and until it became relevant to the case she wouldn't.

It was something of a shock to realize that even in the short time she had been among them the Harvey Girls had inspired a sense of loyalty and camaraderie such that she would not willingly betray one of what was now her own.

Harvey added, "And on the whole they are a capable, loyal bunch." A sigh. "On the whole." He stirred. "You said you had some things to report."

She pulled her attention back to her job. "A few, yes. You said the Express had been robbed three times before this last time."

"Yes. In April, August, and October of last year, February of this year. Four times in all."

"Each the night of the full moon."

"Makes it easier to see what you're doing when you rob a train," he said drily.

"And that each time the cars containing your goods and supplies were targeted."

"Yes."

She kept her voice steady and without any hint of accusation. "Did you look beyond those thefts?"

She felt him stiffen. "Beyond? What do you mean?"

"Did you examine your accounts prior to the train robberies?"

"Explain." His voice was cold and devoid of any remnant of humor.

"You have a line item in your chart of accounts for pilferage."

"Of course. Every reputable business involved in sales does. It's impossible to eliminate all theft. The best we can do is keep track, try to catch the perpetrators and fire them."

"Not arrest them?"

He shrugged. "For the small thefts we don't bother, and most of them are small amounts. It's the price of doing business."

"Like train robberies."

"A difference in degree, yes, but not in kind."

She was silent for a moment. "What am I doing here, Mr. Harvey? If pilferage, theft, the robberies themselves are all part of the price of doing business, why did you hire the Pinkertons to investigate?"

His voice hardened. "As I said in Chicago, Miss Wright, because one of our employees was murdered. Beheaded, in fact, in an utterly barbaric act, like some character out of one of the ancient Greek plays, and left to die on the ground by the tracks bearing our own cars. The head of the Santa Fe is quite in agreement with me that the murderers must be found and brought to justice, or such justice as is available to us here in the New Mexico Territory."

She could well imagine what that justice would look like. There was no judge in Montaña Roja and the only jury would be enough volunteers to pull on the rope. "But if the conductor was involved in the robberies—"

He interrupted her. "What if he was? Equally, what if he wasn't? Do we just bury him and walk away? Do his murderers get off scot-free? What stops them from killing again? What stops them from declaring open season on any and all employees of the Santa Fe and of the Harvey

Houses, too? No. We are our brother's keeper, Miss Wright. Harry Funston, innocent or guilty, deserves justice."

Harry Funston was dead and wouldn't know if he got justice or not. Clare thought about the young man she'd seen shot down in the street of Montaña Roja, with the sheriff himself standing idly by.

This evening, she'd danced with his killer.

But Clare appreciated Harvey's sentiment, and she was being paid to do a job, after all. "If you go all the way back to the beginning of your operations here, extrapolate the amount entered in the pilferage category from every month's balance sheet and put them in a column, you will find that that amount increases over time."

"Of course it does." Harvey sounded impatient. "Expenses, payroll, capital expenditures increased almost as we were building the House, as we stocked it, as we opened one step at a time, first the newsstand, then the counter, then the dining room. Staff increases exponentially and there is simply no way short of hiring a private army to watch each of them every minute of every day. Kitchens are almost impossible to police, and—" He snorted out an unexpected laugh. "Try telling Chef he can't taste the food he's cooking, Miss Wright. Go ahead. I'll wait, and pick up what's left of you when he's done. It's the least I can do."

She gave a dutiful chuckle but stuck to her point. "I do understand what you are saying, Mr. Harvey. What I am referring to is the figures on your monthly balance sheets. For the first six months, they rose steadily but in small increments. On the seventh month, however, they nearly doubled."

"The seventh month after opening?"

"Yes. The following month they dropped back down again to a more reasonable level."

"Spoilage, possibly? It happens. It's a long way from Kansas City and it can get very hot anywhere you care to name on the high iron. Sometimes the refrigerated cars falter or fail completely."

She shook her head. "Three months later it happened again, and then continued to increase until it stopped."

"When?" But she could tell he knew.

"The month before the first of your trains was robbed."

There was a long silence.

Into it she said, "I think there has been organized theft going on from almost the moment you opened the Montaña Roja Harvey House, Mr. Harvey. I think it started out small, just to test the waters, to see if the company would notice. When it didn't, the thieves got more ambitious and much more creative. Why steal one sack of flour when you can snatch a car full of it and sugar and spices and canned goods and everything else along with it in one grand theft?"

They sat in silence for a long time, neither of them admiring the view as much as they had when they arrived.

When Harvey spoke again his voice was grim. "Louis has to be in on it."

"So long as you're sure he can add."

Harvey said frostily, "All of my House managers can add, Miss Wright."

"Is each House manager responsible for balancing the books of their House?"

"Yes."

"And are they required to draw up a balance sheet at the end of each month?"

"Yes."

"And an income and expense statement?"

He sighed. "Yes."

"And copies are sent to headquarters in Kansas City?"

"Yes." Harvey sounded bleak.

She said regretfully, "Then I'm very much afraid, Mr. Harvey, that you are correct. Mr. Abernathy is in this conspiracy to rob Fred Harvey Company up to his neck."

She paused for a moment's thought. "Further, I would say that Abernathy is one of two employees essential to organize and commit these thefts, the other being the conductor of the train that is to be robbed."

"In this case Harry Funston."

"Yes." She paused. "It may prove helpful to talk to the other conductors on the line, Mr. Harvey."

"Why?" Harvey sounded almost despairing.

"Because Harry Funston might not have been the first conductor to be approached to join in this business, sir, and if that proves to be true, and if it was Abernathy who did the recruiting, it only strengthens the case against him. And that being the case…"

"Yes?"

"It is quite true, Mr. Harvey, that there is no honor among thieves. If we are able to collect enough evidence against Abernathy, we can use that to, ah, persuade him to reveal who else was in the gang."

Harvey was horrified. "Gang? Gang! You think there is some sort of—of cabal, a syndicate, a—a ring of people involved?"

Clare recruited her patience and kept her voice even. "Mr. Harvey, we are talking about thefts of entire freight cars, two, three, four at a time. These were thirty-four-foot cars, each of which could carry a minimum of fifty tons of freight. The thieves did not just make off with the freight; they made off with the cars that carried the freight. They did not just vanish into thin air, like a magic trick in a Ringling Brothers circus act. There would have to have been an engine, and indeed the—what is he called—the hoghead from the last robbery indicated that he had heard another engine. I've written to Mr. Pinkerton to see if he can acquire any witness statements that were taken from the other robberies."

It was beyond her comprehension that this had not already been done, but she forbore to say so. Mr. Harvey was quite disturbed enough already. "From what I have learned of Funston and what I've seen of Abernathy, neither has the capacity to organize a theft on that scale. Whoever is doing this has brains, resources, and manpower. None of the cars have been found, have they?"

"No."

"Has anyone looked for them?"

"Of course. Mr. Pinkerton tasked an agent with that. He has been to every town on the railroad in the northern half of the Territory. He has found nothing, no trace, and no whispers either, which I find even more remarkable."

She was silent for a moment, digesting this. The railroad stretched farther in every direction daily. It was possible that the stolen cars weren't even still in the country. It was a little under six hundred miles to El Paso, and she imagined that Porfirio Díaz's customs agents were even more susceptible to bribes to look the other way than U.S. customs agents were. All it would take was a train schedule to coordinate with the legitimate travel down the tracks.

She stirred. "Brains, resources, manpower, and a pretty effective hideout, then. Mr. Harvey, why wasn't the discrepancy in the books seen in Kansas? Copies of all the records are audited there, or so you said in Chicago."

If possible he sounded even more grim. "I don't know, but I'll find out." He struck his knee in impotent rage. "Do you know the planning involved in ensuring that the same fresh ingredients arrive at every Harvey House every day? We factor in pilferage, yes, but also outright loss and of course spoilage. The refrigerator car is a miraculous invention but even it does us no good if it sits idle in the sun long enough for it to run out of fuel."

"Has that happened?"

"Not yet, no, but if this continues, aided and abetted by our own staff, people who have worked for me for years—years!—it will. If the Santa Fe hears of this they could shut down the entire Harvey House enterprise."

This was a given, as the ATSF was footing Harvey's bill as a promotional effort to entice people to buy tickets on their railroad.

"Why do these people do this? Why? We pay better than anyone else, they eat right off the House menu, they sleep in real beds—some of them better than they ever slept in at home!"

Because they could, she thought. As much attention as he paid to the standards of the Fred Harvey Houses, taking nothing for granted to the extent of dropping in unannounced on Houses to see that those standards were kept, he seemed on occasion to be remarkably innocent in the ways of humankind.

They sat in silence for a moment. There was a flurry of gunshots, distant but distinct. It was unmistakable, a sound like no other. She knew a fervent hope that the only victims were more store windows. "Mr. Harvey—"

"What."

He sounded exhausted and she was sorry for him but she knew her duty. "There will be another full moon this Saturday. The day after tomorrow."

"But they—they couldn't possibly..." His voice died. After a moment he said, "I'm sorry I ever went to see Robert Pinkerton."

She resisted the impulse to give him a comforting pat on the arm. "I don't blame you. Ah—"

"What? What now?"

She didn't bother to sugarcoat it. "My room was searched my first day here."

The view had lost some of its enchantment for both of them.

"Miss Wright?"

"Yes, Mr. Harvey?"

"There is something I neglected to tell you in Chicago."

She took a deep breath and let it out slowly. "What might that be, Mr. Harvey?"

"I had to tell him."

"Tell who?"

"Louis Abernathy. I had to tell him who you were, or well, not exactly..." He rushed on before she could respond, not knowing that her tongue had frozen to the roof of her mouth. "I had to tell him to give you the only single room.

I knew it would help in your work if you could slip out without being observed. He was the only person who could make that happen."

Clare tried very hard to keep any hint of condemnation out of her tone. "He didn't ask why?"

"He did, but I told him he didn't need to know. And," he added wretchedly, "I thought it was safe enough. I didn't believe he was involved."

She said nothing, for fear she would say too much.

He heaved a sigh. "I think I just didn't want to believe he was involved."

Very innocent indeed.

But at least now she knew who had searched her room her first day at the House.

## 8

"And you, sir, are an incorrigible flirt."

### April 3, 1890

### Thursday

She slipped inside the back door of the dance parlor and paused for a moment to allow her eyes to adjust to the darkness.

There was a scuffle in the dark. "No! Let me go!" a female voice said, sounding panicked.

There was a male laugh. "Come on, you knew what I wanted when you agreed to meet me back here."

"No, I didn't, I don't want this, no, please stop!"

"Hello?" Clare said, pitching her voice to be heard. "Is someone there?"

There was a muffled curse and she moved with soundless steps to the lavatory door and slipped inside. Running footsteps sounded outside followed by a slower, heavier tread. She waited another moment before using the facilities and stepping back into the hallway.

"You," a voice said, and she turned to see Abernathy standing too few feet away.

"I beg your pardon?" Clare said, doing her best to look and sound bewildered. "Yes, it's me, Mr. Abernathy," and added helpfully, "The new girl. Clare Wadsworth."

He took a step nearer, close enough for her to feel his breath on her cheek. She stood her ground.

"Very well, Miss *Wadsworth*." He emphasized her name and chuckled. It was a guttural and unpleasant sound. "Whatever your name is, you tend to your business and keep your nose out of mine."

"I'm afraid I don't know what you mean, sir," she said stiffly.

He ran that hot gaze over her, leaving nothing out of his observation. Her skin crawled and she was unable to repress an expression of distaste. He saw it and chuckled again. "Don't worry, Miss *Wadsworth*. You're hands off." He leaned down to whisper in her ear. "For now."

Before she could react he had passed her and when she turned, only the movement of the curtain through which he had passed was evidence of his presence.

She smoothed her hair and tugged at the hem of her jacket, noticing with some pride that her hands weren't shaking. The weight in the hidden pocket resting against her right leg had never felt so comforting.

As she twitched the curtain aside to follow him, she saw Florence at a table with her arm around Ida Sterling, who was visibly upset. Across the room stood Louis Abernathy, looking angry.

She looked for Henrietta and found her on the opposite side of the room, surrounded by eager suitors, her eyes on the man who wasn't one of them. She looked even angrier.

The band struck an opening chord. Someone took her hand and she turned her head to see it was Uncle Fred, also known as the sheriff of Montaña Roja, the man with the star. "May I have this dance, miss?"

He was upright without assistance, his hand was firm but undemanding, and his eyes, while a little bloodshot, were admiring. "I'd be honored, sir."

To her astonishment she was swept across the floor by quite the most graceful partner of the evening. Perfectly on the beat of the song—another Strauss waltz—he held her at the correct distance, his left hand remained at her waist without taking any exploratory trips north or south, and he led her through the steps without seeming to lead at all.

"You are a wonderful dancer, sir," she said after they completed their first circle of the floor.

A smile transformed his face from dour drunk to pleasant middle-aged man fully present in the moment. "Easy enough, ma'am, when one is dancing with a feather."

Clare felt herself actually blush, a reaction she had thought she had cured herself of years since. "You are too kind, sir."

"Not at all." He executed a flawless full circle turn and again she had cause to spare a grateful thought for Vassar, this time for that class in ballroom dancing and for the boys from UNY Poughkeepsie whose toes she had mangled during her first steps on the dance floor. "They tell me you're one of the Harvey Girls."

"I am. I've seen you there at lunch." I've even waited on you, she thought, but you were in no condition then to recognize me now.

He smiled that transformative smile again and for a dazed moment she wondered if the city fathers of Montaña Roja had that very day handed off the sheriff's badge to someone else. She pulled herself together. "You're the sheriff. And you're Uncle Fred."

One-two-three. "And how, miss, would you know that?"

"I heard Bob call you that."

One-two-three. "You know my nephew?"

"I've waited on him, too. At Mr. Gowan's table."

They were the same height and if she hadn't been able to look directly into his eyes she would have missed that sudden change of expression, a lightning shift from charming flirtation to ice-cold calculation that chilled her to the bone. Her hand in his felt trapped, his arm around her waist an iron bar. That sudden trepidation must have shown in her expression because the icy calculation in his vanished at once. "Of course. You are a Harvey Girl. You must have waited on everyone in Montaña Roja by now."

"Very nearly." She took in a deep breath and let it out carefully, hoping he didn't notice the pulse she could feel beating rapidly in her veins. "I understand Bob works for Mr. Gowan."

"Has anyone told you how beautiful your hair is, Miss—" One-two-three.

"Wadsworth, and yes, but thank you. Bob is Mr. Gowan's foreman, I believe."

"Mm." One-two-three.

"Is that how you came to Montaña Roja? Or did you get here first?"

"You're very curious, Miss Wednesday."

"Wadsworth. The name is Wadsworth. What is your family name, Fred?"

The song drew to a close and he ended their dance with a flourish that was as graceful as it was restrained. "Ah," he said, shaking his head, "if I told you that, you'd stop calling me Fred."

She couldn't help laughing. "I will have to resort to finding the sheriff's office and reading the name on the door."

There was that flash of ice again and this time she nearly recoiled from it. She wondered suddenly how much of his drunk act was simply an act.

"Trust you to grab up the prettiest girl in the room, old man." Bob stepped between them and winked at Clare. "Mind if I cut in?"

Fred stepped back with a slight bow. "Thank you for such an enjoyable dance, Miss Wadsworth."

She inclined her head. "You made it so, sir."

Bob danced with less grace than Fred but made up for it with enthusiasm. They nearly collided with Henrietta and the murderer on their first transit of the dance floor.

"What is it, Miss Wadsworth? You looked troubled just then." He had a dimple which was charming but was nowhere near as seductive as his uncle's.

"You know my name, sir? I wonder how, since we have yet to be introduced."

"I heard you tell my uncle as I came up on the two of you." He followed her gaze. "Another of the Harvey Girls, isn't it?"

"A week ago I saw the young man she is dancing with shoot his partner in the street. In broad daylight."

"Welcome to the West, darlin'."

She stared at him. He was the same height and had the same lantern jaw and the same husky build as his uncle, if he did have a lot more hair. "His partner died, Mr...."

"Parker. Bob Parker, darlin', and completely at your service."

Fred Parker, then, she thought, if Fred was a paternal uncle. "He's a murderer, Mr. Parker."

The waltz ended and Bob raised her hand to his lips. "That's our dirty little secret out here in the wild, wild West, darlin'. We're all killers." He winked at her again, by which she deduced that the label didn't bother him much. "Thanks for the dance. You are a lovely partner, darlin'."

"And you, sir, are an incorrigible flirt."

"That I am, darlin', that I am."

"And nowhere near as good a dancer as your uncle."

He laughed. "He was pretty taken with you, too." He kissed her hand and then before she could stop him leaned forward to snatch a quick kiss. He chuckled at her affronted expression—as least she hoped that was the feeling she was conveying—and chucked her under the chin. "Thanks for that, too, darlin'."

Before she could deliver a blistering reproof a spry elf of a man hopped up on stage. He was attired in a tweed suit bagged at elbows and knees, with tufts of white hair standing straight up around a shining bald crown in an unintended, elevated tonsure. This must be Mr. Billingsley, as his first words proved. "Thank you, ladies and gentlemen, on behalf of my wife and myself for a wonderful evening! A round of applause for our splendid band, hailing all the way from Kansas City and points north, the Van Horn Orchestra!"

Applause, cheers, and piercing whistles. The orchestra leader bowed. The elf beamed. "Thank you, thank you, all! And now, Mr. Van Horn, if you will play us out."

The strains to "Home on the Range" were heard and with the elf conducting, the crowd sang along, verse, chorus, and repeat, full throated and word perfect. Next to her, Bob Parker was singing tenor, loudly and ever so slightly off key.

The elf's beam was even brighter as the last "day" faded away. "Thank you for that most spirited rendition, ladies and gentlemen! And now, good night!" There was a round of applause and the crowd began a surge for the door, momentarily bottlenecked as the men paused to pick up their holsters and strap them on. Few of them, Clare noticed, waited to do so until they stepped outside.

Florence came bustling up. "There you are, I thought we'd lost you."

"I'm not surprised. What a crowd!"

"I know, wasn't it wonderful!" Florence beamed and leaned in to speak in a confiding tone. "My father's farm was ten miles from the nearest town. But we could have walked here tonight! It's so exciting!"

"It certainly is," Clare said, watching the killer with whom she had shared a dance strap on his pistol, which he had undoubtedly used to kill his partner. "Florence, tell me something. We're not allowed to do this, are we? Harvey Girls, I mean? Wouldn't we be fired if we were caught sneaking out at night?"

Florence blushed and giggled. "Well, no, of course we're not allowed to, and of course we don't usually when Fred is in residence, and you've seen how careful we are when he is. But—" she waved a hand "—who could say no to all of this!"

"Who indeed."

Florence bridled a little. "I know it's different for you, Clare dear, and for Henrietta, as you were both raised in a town." By then the rest of the staff was well acquainted with Clare Wadsworth's fictional past history.

"Florence, if anything I am delighted at the circumstances in which I find myself. I took the job because I need to make a living and it comes with board and room and pays better than anything else I could find. But I did so under the misapprehension that the job would leave no time for a social life."

Florence brightened. "Of course! Most of the Girls do. I didn't because my elder sister was a Harvey Girl before me and I knew what to expect. Just between you and me and the gatepost, she got me the job. She told them I was eighteen."

Clare laughed. "And you were how old, in truth?"

Florence dimpled. "Sixteen."

Clare shook her head in mock disapproval. "A rule breaker through and through, that's what you are, Florence Sellers."

"I know. Isn't it fun?"

"What happened to your sister?"

"Mabel? She married a railroad man, a conductor." Florence's bright light dimmed. "He died recently, and now she's left with three children, so returning to Harvey Houses is out."

"I'm so sorry to hear it," Clare said. "How did he die?"

Florence leaned forward. "He was murdered. Two months ago."

Clare's heart skipped a beat. "How horrible! What happened? It wasn't in one of those awful gunfights in the street, was it?"

"Oh no." Florence's voice dropped. "His train was robbed. He was a conductor. He must have tried to stop them, because they killed him." Her lips compressed. "I have to say I didn't like him much. He was a little too grabby, you know?"

After two weeks as a Harvey Girl, Clare knew.

"But my sister loved him. That's where I go every day off. With three little ones she can use the extra pair of hands."

Clare said faintly, "She lives close enough that you can visit?"

"Oh yes, she's cooking for Mr. Gowan at his new house. It's about two miles from town. She's a great cook, is our Mabel, but of course all the chefs at Harvey Houses are men. I believe Mr. Harvey secured her the position, as he and Mr. Gowan are the best of friends. Such a kind man, Mr. Harvey. He really looks after his employees."

She bustled off, leaving Clare prey to some uncomfortable thoughts. Chief among them was, why hadn't Harvey told her about Mabel Funston?

In the first place, that she even existed?

It was a Pinkerton maxim, tested and proved, that if one existed, a spouse was always the best source of information on a prospective target. In Bienville, Mississippi, Clare had befriended Mary Calhoun with the specific aim of gaining Mary's confidence so as to gather intelligence on her husband, who had always been the prime suspect in the investigation. Mrs. Calhoun had been delighted at the prospect of a confidante, especially one of the wealth and social stature Clare had invented solely for Mrs. Calhoun's edification.

In the here and now, during her perambulations around Montaña Roja, Clare might have passed Mabel Funston in the street and never have known it, whereas if she had she could have choreographed a meeting.

She could not imagine Robert Pinkerton not making that clear to Fred Harvey as he explained their methods.

# 9

"Drinking on the job?"

"Every chance I get."

April 4, 1890

Friday

Florence was about to have even more fun, as they all discovered the following morning, when Mr. Abernathy called them together in the lull between breakfast and lunch for an announcement from Mr. Harvey, who was still with them.

"Thank you all for coming," Harvey said formally. Abernathy stood at his side, which might have accounted for the fact that Harvey's smile did not reach his eyes.

As agreed between Clare and Harvey, there was not enough proof to show cause to have Abernathy removed from his office, let alone arrested. If Sheriff Parker was ever sober enough to do such a thing. No, it was much better to leave Abernathy where he was, with Clare and now Harvey watching him. He would eventually make a mistake and he would be fairly caught out, and could be encouraged to give up his fellow thieves and bring the organization, for organization it must be, down once and for all.

Or so they hoped, Clare thought.

"You all know Mr. G.W. Gowan, local businessman, as he lunches here practically every day he's in town and dines here often as well," Harvey said. "As I'm sure you've heard he has built himself a new home in the foothills of the Sangre de Cristos, on the Rio Roja a few miles south of town. This Saturday he is hosting an at-home for the citizens of Montaña Roja. The doors will open at noon and Mr. Gowan will leave them open, he says, until the food and drink run out or everyone goes home. We all know which will happen first."

A titter ran around the room and he smiled again, more naturally this time.

"I wish we could go," Florence whispered.

Whisper or not, Harvey heard her. "You may wish otherwise, Miss Sellers. As it happens, I have good news and bad news for you and for the rest of the girls."

An exchange of glances and excited whispers.

"The good news is, you're getting tomorrow off. The House in Trinidad will pack meals for those passengers on that day's express who are traveling through Montaña Roja. The Montaña Roja House—" he waved an all-inclusive hand "—will be closed for the day."

Gasps all around.

"The bad news is, you'll be the ones serving the food and drink at Mr. Gowan's at-home."

A stunned but only momentary silence. "We get to go to the open house!" "We get to see the house first!" And, inevitably, "Are we getting paid for this?" Elizabeth, of course.

Harvey grinned. "Not by me, Miss Higgins." He waited for a moment, allowing the dismay to gather on their faces, and then added smoothly, "The expense of your salaries for the day will be borne by Mr. Gowan himself, and—" he held up a hand to forestall their comments "—he invites you to be there an hour before the doors open, when he will be delighted to escort you personally over the house, for your own private tour."

The response was all he could have hoped for, and that night there was an orgy of washing and ironing and of tying each other's hair up in rags. Florence, a blonde, appropriated a lemon from the kitchen and used the juice on her hair. Everyone rubbed their hands with a bit of the precious lotion made from their mother's secret recipe and wore cotton gloves to bed.

Gowan sent a buckboard lined with bench seats and at ten thirty they were jolting down the rudimentary one-lane road that had provided access for the men who laid the track for the railroad. After twenty minutes they came to a turnoff which led to another, much better maintained dirt road, one with all the potholes graded out. This road led through pastures fenced with barbed wire, enclosing a scattered collection of red-and-white shorthorn cattle just beginning to drop their calves. The Rio Roja glittered in the distance, reflecting the rays of the morning sun, and along its banks tall cottonwoods were greening up with new leaves. Ponderosa pines darkened the foothills, the contrast turning the already deep blue sky into sapphire, as if the heavens above were themselves carved from one continuous gemstone.

"Those calves look so sweet," someone said.

"Sure," Florence said, "real sweet, so long as you don't have to milk them when they grow up," and everyone laughed.

The road wound its way through the cottonwoods and crossed a small wooden bridge over the river. Clare looked down into the water and saw that it had a reddish tinge. She looked up again at the Sangre de Cristos (it was seldom possible to look away from them) and imagined a seam of iron ore deep in a narrow crevice of granite being continually washed down from where that stream rose at the head of some distant valley. She would have liked to have followed the river back to the source to see it with her own eyes.

Next to her Florence gasped and she sat up. "Look!"

Clare followed her pointing finger. If she were ruthlessly honest with herself she would have to admit that her own jaw dropped, just a little.

She had spent brief visits, professionally, including the case she had worked with Bat, in more than one of the new mansions going up in Chicago over the last two decades since the Great Chicago Fire. She was familiar with the American nouveau riche's determination to lay on as much as the traffic would bear in the way of ornamentation, in their own persons, in their transportation, in their office buildings, but particularly in the construction of their homes. She'd been unable to avoid learning some of the names of the different styles, Romanesque, Richardsonian, Châteauesque, Second Empire, Victorian, the ever popular Greek Revival.

She had never, until this moment, seen one structure attempt to encompass them all. A.J. Calhoun would have died on the spot of sheer envy.

There were two turrets on each front corner and a central tower over the massive set of doors. There was a row of Doric columns holding up a portico, although why Gowan's architect would have balked at the more ornate Corinthian was a mystery. The windows on the first floor had Roman arches; on the second floor the windows were Gothic. The facing stone on the first floor was even slabs of a rough, irregular flagstone with a golden tint; the second floor was faced with what looked to be cobblestones made of the same stone.

"Rusticated," she said.

"What?" Florence said.

"The style. The way the stones on the wall are placed, big rectangles on the bottom, smaller knobbly ones on the top. Rusticated."

Florence looked at her askance. "If you say so."

Clare smiled. "My parents had a friend who was an architect. He used to take us to tea in the Adelphi Hotel on Sunday afternoons and tell us all about what he was working on at the time."

A lie from start to finish but Florence was duly reassured that her new friend harbored no abnormal interest in a profession not open to women. At least Clare hoped she was. She liked Florence and it was sometimes difficult to mind her tongue in the other Girl's presence.

The roof between the tower and the turrets was flat, and here and there the leafy tops of trees waved gently over the edge. Clare was guessing a roof garden.

There wasn't so much as a single block of adobe anywhere to be seen. So, she thought, no concessions made to local aesthetics, then. Just sheer, unadulterated Gilded Age excess. Mark Twain could have used it as a model for Silas Hawkins' dream house.

Over the doors was an elaborately keyed cornice, surmounted by an honest-to-god pediment. Inside the pediment on the left was a bas-relief of Zeus, if the bolt of lightning in his raised right hand was any indication. On the left was an actual motto, carved into the stone itself.

*Voluntatem meam.*
*Fortitudo mea.*
*Iter meum.*

Clare had had Latin forced upon her by the Quakers and Vassar both and she did not recognize this motto from any of the texts. Gowan must have made up his own.

How very Caesarian of him.

She felt a giggle rising in her throat and suppressed it ruthlessly. Florence did cast her a questioning look. Clare raised her eyebrows and her shoulders and Florence shrugged and went back to adoring Wash Gowan's monument to his own greatness.

He waited for his guests at the top of the broad staircase that led to the door, dressed in what looked like the same suit he'd been wearing on the train. He didn't look anything at all like Julius Caesar but the resemblance to

Andrew Carnegie and John Jacob Astor and J.P. Morgan, at least in an "I am the secular lord thy god" attitude, was unmistakable.

She didn't like him, she realized, and wondered why. He was sufficiently handsome, well-mannered, affable to a chance-met stranger on a train, interested in an attractive woman without being obnoxious, and no question that he had succeeded in business, as witness this American-style Mad King Ludwig castle he'd built for himself. Every woman would fall instantly in love with him; every man would want to be him. He would expect no less.

*My will. My strength. My way.* If her Latin held up this was the literal translation of the motto engraved on the pediment, the one he was standing beneath, before the magnificent double doors through which they were all about to parade. She hoped he didn't take the motto literally as regards his guests.

"Welcome to Gowan House, and thank you all so much for helping me out here today." He turned to clap a hand on Fred Harvey's shoulder. "The Harvey House is a good neighbor. Never let it be said the neighbors don't appreciate it!"

Gowan smiled suddenly and there was the friendly man she'd met between the cars coming into town. He could put that persona on like a warm coat. She wondered how many other personas he had stored in the same closet.

"Please, come in," he said. "Reyes will take your things."

They deposited their outwear with the stout, impassive Indian lady at the door. "Thank you," Clare said, but there was no response in the woman's black eyes. Clare wondered if she were deaf.

The interior lived up to the exterior, a Beaux-Arts dream come true. There was a grand entrance that took up most of the front third of the ground floor, with an equally grand staircase with oak banisters whose uprights were carved in the draped shapes of caryatids. Their footsteps echoed off great squares of polished granite. On the right was a library with three walls of bookshelves made from more oak and a massive wooden escritoire that Clare coveted on sight. On the left was a parlor lined with tall, narrow arched windows which was filled with furniture acquired from, variously, the courts of Victoria, Louis XIV, and Emperor Tongzhi. Both rooms had double pocket doors that could be drawn back to form one great room with the grand entrance. Gowan demonstrated, and Florence, laughing, curtsied to him and held out her hand. "A dance, kind sir?"

"But we have no music, miss." They took a turn around the room nonetheless, to general applause. Fred Harvey positively glowed.

There was a dining room that could seat fifty at a polished oak refectory table set with two silver candelabra with so many arms they looked like Hindu deities. Upstairs, half the doors were locked, but Gowan had left some of the bedrooms open. Each was a suite with its own bath, each beautifully furnished in some iconic period.

Elizabeth paused next to Clare, who stood staring into one. "Looks like Marie Antoinette just stepped out, doesn't it?"

Clare nodded. "On her way to the guillotine. Let them eat cake!"

They both snickered.

As Clare reached the bottom of the stairs Florence grabbed her hand. "Come on, I want to introduce you to Mabel."

She pulled Clare toward the back, where a massive kitchen took up most of the rear of the house.

Mabel was Florence plus a few years, plus three children, plus a recent widowing. There were silver hairs over her ears and her eyes were tired, although they lit up when they saw Florence. "Florrie!"

"Mabel, love, I just wanted to introduce you to our newest girl. Miss Clare Wadsworth, my sister, Mrs. Mabel Funston."

Clare held out her hand and Mabel held up both of hers, which were covered in flour up to the elbows. The three of them laughed together. "It's good to meet you, Miss Wadsworth."

"Oh, make it Clare, please."

"And Mabel."

Clare cast an admiring glance around the kitchen, filled with all the newest appliances, including the largest stove she had ever seen outside the Harvey House kitchen. There was even a bar set up on one side with two bartenders on duty backed by a massive cabinet filled with delectable-looking bottles. "This must be a wonderful place to work. All the modern conveniences one could wish for." She spotted the sink, the width of the counter and four feet long. Instead of the more rurally common pump handle it had a faucet. "And running water!"

"Hot and cold," Mabel said proudly.

"Such luxury in a private home!"

"Especially here," Clare said.

"I know, and believe me when I say how much I appreciate it. When Mr. Harvey found me this job I was afraid I would be hauling water from a well. But Mr. Gowan insisted on the best of everything, all of it modern and up to date." She cast a harried look at the clock on the wall. "I'm sorry, but I really must get these pastries into the oven. I'm so sorry, Florrie, there is just no time to visit today."

"I can only imagine, Mabel dear. We have to get to work, too."

"I know," Clare said, as if inspiration had just struck, "when do you next get into town, Mabel? We three could meet at the coffeehouse on Third and Jefferson."

"Oh, but that's a wonderful idea, Mabel, yes, let's please do that!" Florence said, casting Clare a grateful look.

Mabel looked doubtful. "The children—"

"Surely you can find someone to sit with them for a few hours." Florence caught her sister's hand, flour and all. "Please. Take a little time for yourself."

A voice said, "Shall we get on with it, ladies?"

Clare looked around and saw Abernathy standing watching them with a frown on his face.

"Sorry, Mr. Abernathy." She reached for a tray loaded with oysters on the half shell and headed for the door.

Florence instantly followed her, so closely she trod on Clare's heel. "Sorry, sir."

Perforce Abernathy must give way before them but his stare was inimical, Clare thought deliberately so. She met it with a bland expression. "Excuse me, sir."

In the hallway she met Fred Harvey, who spoke to her in a low voice. "Keep your eyes open today."

A totally unnecessary instruction she found annoying, but she nodded. As she came through the door into the great room she saw Gowan watching both of them.

Really, if she thought about it too hard she would begin to consider herself irresistible.

"Oh, that looks delicious! May I?"

She turned to see the plump matron she had seen sashay out of the clothing store, wearing her new plaid dress.

"Certainly, ma'am."

The next hours passed in a blur of faces, orders of drinks without end, and the constant weight of a tray on her shoulder. No one in Montaña Roja was going to miss the opportunity of walking through Wash Gowan's new mansion, and there was a goodly representation from neighboring communities as well.

She served lemonade to Lieutenant Colonel Benteen and his wife, and a stein of beer to Magistrate Platt. Sheriff Parker took his whiskey neat and continually. Bob Parker tried to strike up a conversation and she shoved the last mixed drink she had on her tray (it was green) into his hand and went hurrying back to the kitchen for another tray of Mabel's delectable snacks, on the way passing Wash Gowan, who smiled at her and mouthed the words "Thank you" as she passed. Dr. Irwin, Montaña Roja's only doctor, asked for a Sazerac, from the twinkle in his eye a challenge to the bartender, who met it with ease, and Fred Harvey was drinking lemonade. It was good lemonade, too; Clare had sampled some in the kitchen.

"Martini, two olives," someone said in her ear, and she turned to see Bat Masterson at her side, elegant as ever in his tailored suit.

"Drinking on the job?"

"Every chance I get," he said cheerfully, and she dutifully fetched him his martini. It was served in a water glass. He raised it to take a drink and paused. "Butch." Voice and face both were devoid of expression, eyes watchful.

She looked around to see Bob Parker standing behind her with an equally void expression as he looked at Masterson. His hand drifted toward his holster. "It's Bob hereabouts. Bartholomew."

"My mistake." Bat raised his glass in an easy salute. "Apologies."

Parker let the side of his jacket cover his holster again. "No harm done." He winked at Clare and then froze in place, looking past Bat.

Clare looked around to see Tom Horn standing a few feet away, holding a frosty glass of lemonade. He bent his head courteously in Clare's direction. "Ma'am. Boys." He moved off.

Parker took in a great gulp of air. "Jesus fucking Christ. What in all the seven rings of hell is he doing here?"

"I need another drink," Bat said.

A bit later Clare was privileged to be within earshot when Sheriff Parker encountered Tom Horn. They both paused, exchanged clearly measuring looks, nodded briefly.

"Tom. Been a while."

"John. You look sober."

"It happens."

"Good to know."

They moved past each other, leaving Clare wondering how many different names the Parker males had, and why.

There were hundreds of people from every walk of Montaña Roja life, and much could be discerned from their state of both sobriety and dress. Those miners who worked the Argentine, Gowan's mine, had made an effort to arrive sober, although they did their best to make up for that at the free bar. Independent miners seemed to be competing with each other as to the amount of accumulated mud on their overalls. It was difficult to distinguish a winner. Clare knew a moment's pity for whoever had to clean up at the end of the day and only hoped it wasn't the Harvey Girls.

Miners, cowboys, clerks, farmers, ranchers both cattle and sheep, husbands and wives dressed in their Sunday best. Clare did recognize one couple from the dance parlor. The husband smiled and said, "How do, miss." The wife scowled and looked away.

Inevitably she overheard bits of conversation not necessarily meant for her ears.

"—she was on his arm in the middle of the day on Jefferson Avenue, and in that gaudy red dress, too! His poor wife—"

"—that vein's about dried up but I saw some color in the north tunnel that makes me think—"

"—only about five, six hunnerd mile from here to Mexico and the railroad runs there right through El Paso and them Mexicans eat as much beef as we do—"

"—sheep regularly have twins or triplets, you can breed them more than once a year, you can sell the wool, and you can eat 'em. I don't care what the Cattleman's Association says, I'm agonna buy me a few head—"

"—waste of another perfectly good full moon—"

"Keep your voice down, for chrissake."

Clare looked around at that but the house was so crowded at this point that she couldn't see who had said it. Bob Parker was standing nearby, the sheriff next to him. Louis Abernathy was facing them with his back to her, and she couldn't tell if he had been either of the people speaking.

Bob noticed her attention and of course he winked at her. She was beginning to think it was a nervous tic.

"—that Díaz is a man you can do business with and it looks like he's got a holt of them revolutionaries now—"

"—Gowan and the rest got all the leases tied up around these parts, thinking it might be smart to head north, might still be some gold or silver left hasn't been found yet, I'm thinking of taking the train up to Trinidad and striking out for western Colorado—"

"—imagine working on your own, away from family, no parental supervision, can you imagine what those girls get up to—"

A Mexican grandee magnificent in tight-fitting jacket and trousers embroidered with gold thread stalked in and surveyed the company down a nose that seemed to elongate in the process. He strode over to Gowan and tried to engage him in conversation. Gowan raised a hand, forestalling him, as he continued to talk to a matron in an eye-stinging chartreuse dress with an enormous bustle and what looked like an entire stuffed great blue heron on her hat. The grandee was unaccustomed to attention being paid to anyone other than himself and stalked off again. In motion he looked a little like the heron must have alive.

He was tall enough to see over most of the people there and spotted Lieutenant Colonel Benteen. He stalked in that officer's direction, where Clare was refilling their lemonade glasses. She had waited on them at the restaurant and Mrs. Benteen was pleased to chat for a few moments, although she fell silent when the grandee approached.

"*Coronel*," he said.

The colonel inclined his head. He didn't introduce his wife, who pretended to be invisible. Clare already was invisible to the grandee so she didn't expect a salutation. She took her time filling Mrs. Benteen's glass.

"I must speak to you, *coronel*. The shipments, they are too small and too few."

"Not here and not now, *señor*," the colonel said, and took his wife's arm to steer her away.

The altitudinous gentleman didn't quite stamp his foot in annoyance but it was close. He stalked off, and shortly afterward Clare saw him leaving through the massive set of front doors, held open for him by Bob Parker. Those shut safely behind him; Parker looked at Gowan, who was standing in front of the library fireplace. Gowan nodded, and Parker tossed off a careless salute.

"Who was that man?" she heard someone whisper.

"Who? Oh, the Mexican grandee? That, my dear, is a relative of Porfirio Díaz's wife, one Gabriel Romero Rubio y Castelló."

"My, he sounds very grand. How do you know him?"

"Oh, I don't know him, my dear. Señor Rubio y Castelló does not deign to know people of my status." A grunt. "All right, all right. He stays at the hotel quite often."

"Why?"

"I assume he has business interests here. God knows enough American businessmen have interests on his side of the border."

Early in the afternoon, in a moment that would live with her forever, Clare came face to face with Samuel Langhorne Clemens, known to the literary world as Mark Twain.

She recognized him instantly, of course, as any literate American would have, as indeed anyone who had ever seen the front page of a newspaper in the last ten years would have. But she, an experienced investigator, a woman who took professional pride in maintaining a calm, even demeanor in any situation…

… goggled. She stammered when she was able to speak again. Her voice even went up when she said his name, a thing she was embarrassed by all over again every time she remembered it. "M—Muh—Mr.—Mr. Clemens?"

"Why, yes, ma'am," he said with the hint of a bow, immaculate in his iconic white suit and black bow tie. She realized she had seen him step down from the very train she had come in on herself and that she had somehow failed to recognize the hair. "And you I know by your uniform as a Harvey Girl." The way he said it made it sound as if he thought he were addressing a duchess.

"I am," she said, feeling flattered to be labeled as what she had until this very moment regarded as an epithet.

"A fine group of people, working for a fine organization." He gave her shoulder an avuncular pat with a hand holding the omnipresent cigar. He looked over her shoulder and brightened. "Fred Harvey, as I live and breathe!"

"How are you, Clemens?"

They shook hands with great cordiality. "All the better for seeing you, Harvey, even if I did arrive behind one of your confounded steam engines, belching cinders the whole way. Stagecoaching is infinitely more delightful."

"Yes, yes, I know," Harvey said soothingly, "we are the devil's work. What are you doing here in Montaña Roja?"

"I was in Missouri on business, and I thought I'd just keep on down the road a bit, see what's changed since I was last through this part of the country."

"What has?"

"Everything. Most of which is your fault."

"Guilty as charged." Both men laughed. "We might drink to that."

Clemens chuckled. "As you know, I never refuse to take a drink, under any circumstance."

"I do know that." Harvey looked at Clare. "A drink for Mr. Clemens, Miss Wadsworth?"

Clare got her tongue back into working order. "Certainly, Mr. Harvey. What would you like, Mr. Clemens?"

"Well now, would your bar run to a nice Scotch whiskey, Harvey?"

Harvey nodded at Clare, who, relieved to discover that her legs still worked, returned shortly with the whiskey in a crystal tumbler and a refill for Harvey's lemonade.

Clemens saluted them both and drank. He smacked his lips. "Excellent, Harvey, excellent."

"Where are you staying, Clemens? The town is bursting at the seams but I can find you a room."

Clemens waved his glass. "No need, no need, Harvey. I met Gowan on the train and he kindly offered me a room here." His eyes twinkled. "It has been an experience, I must say."

Harvey looked around to see if Gowan was anywhere near. He leaned forward and spoke in a low voice. "A bit… elaborate, isn't it."

Clemens took his time lighting his cigar. He puffed out a leisurely cloud of smoke. "Oh, my dear Harvey. I have often observed how narrowing a thing it is for a man to have wealth who makes a god of it instead of a servant."

Unable to find an excuse to linger Clare made a sort of bobbing curtsy—she couldn't help herself—and took her empty tray to the kitchen to load up with more snacks. Mr. Clemens might be hungry.

## 10

"They're already starting to call it
the Billion-Dollar Congress, Travers."

*Gowan House*

April 5, 1890

Saturday

Florence seized her. "Clare! Is that who I think it is?"

Clare couldn't stop the smile from spreading across her face. "Yes, it is, if you think he's Samuel Langhorne Clemens, known to us common folk as Mr. Mark Twain."

"And you got to wait on him!"

"It was an accident. I almost walked right into him."

Florence sighed. "Lucky accident! Lucky girl!"

"Well, here then." Clare handed her a loaded tray. "Mr. Clemens might be hungry."

"You're a sweetheart!" Florence shouldered the tray and vanished through the swinging doors.

"That was a nice thing to do," Mabel said, pulling baking trays from an oven the size of a small cavern.

"She's saving me from making a fool of myself," Clare said with a laugh, which might have been the first strictly true thing she had said since stepping down from the train at Montaña Roja Station. It was an odd feeling, and entirely out of character for both her personas, real and invented. You didn't go far in the Pinkertons without the ability to lie with conviction.

She finished loading another tray and sallied back into the fray, where she found Father Cristóbal going at it with Mr. Clemens, who was heard to say, "Ours is a terrible religion, Father. The fleets of the world could swim in spacious comfort in the innocent blood it has spilt."

There was a collective gasp as shocked as it was delighted from the group of people clustered as near to the great man as they could get, of which attention Clare judged both men to be well aware.

Father Cristóbal laughed out loud. "Heretic!"

Clemens bowed in gracious acceptance of the title.

Father Cristóbal wagged a finger. "Yet I must forgive you, so I may in turn be forgiven."

Clemens cocked an eyebrow. "St. Matthew, I believe."

The good father shook his head in mock sadness. "We must reform you, Mr. Clemens, so you have some hope of heaven."

"The church is always trying to get other people to reform," Clemens said. "It might not be a bad idea to reform itself a little, by way of example."

Another collective gasp. The debaters and their audience were all thoroughly enjoying themselves.

Someone waved at Clare and she was obliged to leave them to it.

On the whole people behaved pretty well, in spite of the severe inroads made on the stock of alcohol. The only heated conversations Clare overheard were about the proposed McKinley Tariff. "Fifty percent! Is he serious? Does he know how much it will raise prices on goods and services? Christ! Oh, pardon my language, ma'am. I didn't see you there." The thickset, red-faced man raised his beer stein in apology.

"No need, sir," she said, and as she passed them heard the other man say soothingly, "I believe the gentleman from Ohio means his tariff to protect domestic industries from foreign competition, Manley. That can't be a bad thing, surely."

"It is if it triples the price of a case of canned beans! My boys live on the stuff! Cheap tin is the only reason I can afford to feed them!" A noisy gulp. "They're already starting to call it the Billion-Dollar Congress, Travers. Mark my words, if the Republicans go through with this tariff nonsense they'll be out on their ears in November and Cleveland'll be back in in '92!"

A few other arguments progressed to fistfights but these were either defused or nudged outside by Bob, who employed a mixture of humor and diplomacy that won Clare's respect. At least no outright brawls erupted and since everyone was as usual armed, that could be chalked up as a minor miracle. Harvey looked relieved after each incident. Gowan maintained his usual sangfroid but he had to be pleased that no one had put a bullet through one of his stained glass windows.

She was clearing up some used dishes when she discovered Sheriff John or Fred Parker snoring gently beneath his hat in a chair tucked into a corner of the library. She resisted the urge to kick him in the shins, but only because people might see. What she didn't understand was why none of the city fathers in attendance took on that chore themselves.

By early evening the crowd had thinned. Father Cristóbal had taken a cordial leave of Mr. Clemens. Those who had availed themselves too liberally at the free bar were helped into wagons and carted off. Some were unconscious and were harvested from prone positions behind pieces of furniture inside and ornamental shrubbery outside. Others were mobile but singing in less than harmony.

"All right, people, time to put it to bed," Harvey said.

"No, Fred." Gowan came forward. "Your folks have done more than enough. My thanks to all of you for making this event an unqualified success. Collect the rest of the food and bring it into the parlor, and the bartenders will pour everyone their drink of choice."

"Gowan for president," someone said.

Gowan laughed and said with a twinkle, "Not yet, sir. Not quite yet."

Clare couldn't tell if he was joking or not.

He waved toward the back of the house. Half a dozen Indian women who looked nearly related to Reyes moved in on silent feet and began to clear away the detritus.

Clare went back into the kitchen, where Mabel was already assembling trays full of leftovers. "I do hope you can meet Florence and me in town. You look as if you could use some time off."

"Couldn't I just," Mabel said with feeling.

Clare carried a tray into the parlor, where the Harvey staff crowded in two to a chair and lined the window seats and ate hungrily and drank thirstily.

Clare, from one of the window seats, saw a shadow in the hall from the corner of her eye and looked around to see an Indian woman pass the doorway, cleaning supplies in hand.

"From the San Ildefonso Pueblo," Gowan said from beside her.

She repressed a start. "Oh, I see. They're your cleaning staff?"

"Part-time. Some of the men work in the stables and on the home farm full-time. I can use the help, and they can use the money." He paused. "You and your people did a Trojan's job today, Miss Wadsworth."

"It was our pleasure, Mr. Gowan. As you and Mr. Harvey say, we want to be good neighbors."

"My friends call me Wash, Miss... Wadsworth." He raised an eyebrow, clearly hoping for permission to use her Christian name.

She looked across the room at Fred Harvey, in conversation with Mr. Abernathy. "I don't know that Mr. Harvey would approve of me addressing one of Montaña Roja's leading citizens, not to mention his good friend, his business partner, and one of his best customers with such familiarity."

Gowan chuckled. "Nonsense. Fred is happy with whomever I choose to call me whatever I please."

Fred Harvey must have heard him because he turned to see the two of them standing together. He frowned at her, she thought proving her point. Clare used the momentary distraction to collect a tray full of empty glasses and plates and escape back into the kitchen. Mabel was untying her apron and smoothing back her hair. "A long day," Clare said.

Mabel looked weary. "Very."

"Florence tells me you have three children."

The other woman brightened. "Two sons and a daughter. Four, three and two."

Clare couldn't imagine the horror of caring for three children of below school age alone but she knew the correct response. "Congratulations."

"Thank you. You're not married?"

Clare chuckled. "I live in hope." She didn't but again, she understood her audience and the answer she expected.

"You're pretty enough, not that that matters in the New Mexico Territory. There are so few single women in these parts that even if you were the bearded lady at the circus you'd have to beat them off with a stick." Mabel folded her apron. "You had to sign the contract, though. Like Florence. That you wouldn't marry for at least six months if Fred Harvey hired you."

"Yes." Clare shrugged. "I'm in no hurry. This is such an adventure."

"You've never been to the West before?"

Two of the women from the San Ildefonso Pueblo entered the kitchen. Still silent and still without making eye contact, one collected the mound of soiled linen napkins into a basket and departed. The other filled the wash basin—hot water from the tap, in the New Mexico Territory in 1890, Clare couldn't help but marvel—and began to stack the dirty dishes in proper order of cleaning: glassware, flatware, dinnerware. Mabel watched with a sharp eye.

"No," Clare said, answering Mabel's question. "It is an extraordinary place."

"Extraordinary?" Mabel thought that over. "I suppose it is. We're from Kansas, Florence and I. I'm used to more rain. Or any rain, for that matter. And more green."

"Where do you live?"

"Since we're so far from town Mr. Gowan requires the full-time help to live on the property. Because of the children, we have a small house." She nodded at the woman washing the dishes. "Reyes' daughter Juanita minds the children while I'm at work, at Mr. Gowan's expense."

"Kind," Clare said.

"Necessary. Since my husband—" She stopped.

"Florence mentioned you had recently lost your husband. I am so sorry."

Mabel sighed. "It has been... difficult."

"I can only imagine."

"Well." Mabel raised her chin. "Well, then. What's done is done." She was about to say more when she looked up and stiffened.

Clare looked over her shoulder to see Louis Abernathy pushing through the swinging door. "Cleanup is still in progress, Miss Wadsworth. I'm sure you must have heard something about it."

"Of course, Mr. Abernathy." Clare collected an empty tray and slipped past him into the hallway. She paused long enough to poke her head into the parlor. "The boss is on the prowl."

Ida raised her head with an exaggerated groan. "I thought the Indians were taking care of cleanup?"

"I think he thinks we should be, too." And Clare wanted an excuse to go over the house one more time.

Ida got to her feet with another groan, followed by Florence, Elizabeth, and the stewards. Everyone looked as tired as Clare felt but they went back to work without complaint. They were mostly silent, too, having run out of energy and conversation both after the long day, which exactly suited Clare's humor. The silence and the routine work gave her time to think.

She wondered at the expression she had seen in Mabel's eyes when she looked up to see Abernathy in the doorway. It had looked to Clare very much like hatred, or at the least an intense dislike. Why?

She could think of several reasons if she used her imagination. The most obvious one was that Abernathy didn't restrict his attentions to single women. Either that or he had not wasted time after Funston's death to press them on Mabel.

It seemed, too, that Fred Harvey had been keeping watch on who she spoke with, or at least when she spoke with Gowan. Why? She'd been hired to ferret out the person or persons who had either orchestrated or assisted in the robberies of his trains and the murder of an ATSF employee closely concerned with freight destined for Harvey Houses. Why would he concern himself with who she chose to speak to? Surely that would be as expected as it was necessary to solving the case?

Gowan, too, was keeping a closer eye on her than she was comfortable with, but that she could put down to his interest in an attractive woman. Couldn't she? As Mabel had so astutely pointed out, men outnumbered women in the American Southwest between ten and twenty to one, depending on how remote the location. She'd heard that in some California mining towns ninety-seven percent of the population was male. She could only imagine how exhausted the three percent of the female population must be.

She thought of the foot traffic of Montaña Roja, and of the crowd that had flocked to the dance parlor. The women at the dance parlor had been in continuous demand with the many single men standing around the wall waiting their turn, and the men lucky enough to have a woman on their arm were definitely in the minority. During her short time in Montaña Roja she herself had already fielded a dozen proposals of marriage, an alarming proportion of which were only half in jest, and there was a new story told among the Harvey Girls about an awkward proposal, either honorable or indecent, after every serving at the House.

The light was fading outside, which meant the inside of the house was growing dimmer. The lamps had yet to be lit, which made it all the easier for Clare to glide from room to room. Clare made sure to try all the doors that had been locked on their tour that morning. "Just in case someone was wandering around where they shouldn't be," she told Florence. "Wet glasses leave rings on wooden surfaces and I'd hate to see that happen on our watch."

"No indeed," Florence said with an absolute sincerity that should have made Clare ashamed of her own duplicity, but didn't. "But don't forget Mark Twain himself is probably behind one of them."

They took care to try the door handles as silently as possible, and found glassware and dishes and used napkins discarded on any available horizontal surface or on the floor, hidden behind curtains. A saucer holding two oysters, one chewed, one not, was found in a half-open drawer.

A cigar had been stubbed out on the rim of a bathtub. Clare ran her finger around the inside of the tub and inspected the soap scum that had accumulated on the tip of her finger. "Did someone actually take a bath here this afternoon?"

Florence sighed and shook her head. "We'd better tell one of the housekeepers. At least it isn't Mr. Gowan's own bathroom." Mr. Gowan's own suite having been behind one of the locked doors.

"Wise even before the fact, Mr. Gowan."

"That is his reputation." Florence stretched her back. "This has been fun but, oh, how I want my bed."

"Me, too," Clare said untruthfully.

They came downstairs again and began to chase down errant crockery and other related detritus in the downstairs rooms, splitting up to cover more territory that much more quickly.

Which was how Clare alone found Henrietta in the darkest corner of the library in close conversation with Mr. Abernathy, who looked as if he wished he were anywhere else. Clare moved toward them, finding the odd glass and plate and napkin here and there excuse enough.

Henrietta sounded furious. "What is wrong with you? Why are you acting like this? I've done everything you asked of me, even—"

"Calm down. I told you—"

"I know what you told me! And I know what you promised! I don't want to spend the rest of my life waiting tables! I want a husband and a home and children! You said you wanted the same!"

Clare bumped her toe on an ornate Louis XIV armchair and they both looked around and saw her. "We'll talk later,"

Abernathy said, and left the room precipitously. Henrietta scowled at Clare, and then spoiled the effect by whisking out a handkerchief.

"I do apologize," Clare said gently. "I didn't mean to intrude."

A kind word was all it took for Henrietta to dissolve into a flood of tears. "He made promises. I don't—I can't—I don't know what to do!" She plumped down into a chair. Clare went to the door and closed it. Setting the tray aside she crouched down on the floor next to the weeping woman. She had discovered it was always useful to give a witness the illusion of power by looking down at their interrogator, especially when the witness had no idea she was being interrogated. "What's the matter, Henrietta? How can I help?"

It was the second oldest of stories, the man wanting, the woman wanting marriage, the woman offering her body as a guarantor of formal status, the man uninterested after he'd gotten what he wanted. "I thought he loved me," Henrietta sobbed. "He said he did, and I believed him, and now he—he—"

Clare had an unwontedly vivid recollection of the scene in Abernathy's office. And now he, indeed.

"I did everything he asked of me, even—" Henrietta caught herself and stared at Clare through tear-filled eyes, her lip caught between her teeth.

Clare did her best to look bewildered. "Even what?"

The door opened behind her and Henrietta leapt to her feet, but it was only Ida, who peered curiously around the door at the two of them. "All done in here? Why, Henrietta, whatever is the matter?" She sounded less sincere than curious, and Clare remembered the scene she had heard backstage in the dance parlor.

Henrietta blew her nose and tucked her handkerchief back in her sleeve. "Nothing," she said. "Nothing at all." She marched past Ida and through the door with her nose in the air, spoiling the effect when she tripped over the edge of the carpet.

"What was all that about?" Ida said.

Clare got to her feet. "I haven't the least idea." She reached for her tray, and made a show of hesitation. "I think—" she glanced at the other girl "—I think it might have something to do with Mr. Abernathy."

Ida snorted. "I'll bet it does."

"Whatever do you mean?"

Ida remembered that she wanted to keep her job. "Nothing. Nothing at all. Just stay out of his reach, is my advice."

"Ah." Clare looked wise. "Grabby?"

"Just—" Ida hesitated "—just take care never to be alone in a room with him."

"One more pass through all the open rooms, ladies," Harvey said from the doorway. "Mr. Gowan was very kind to bring in help for the cleanup but I think he underestimated the amount of guests he would have." He made a face. "Or the mess they would leave behind. The least we can do is clear it away so the cleaning ladies can get to it. Start upstairs and work down, and please take every care to do so quietly. Mr. Clemens has retired to his room and may be asleep."

"Yes, Mr. Harvey."

Clare took the opportunity to use the downstairs lavatory designated that day for the public, after which she returned her loaded tray to the kitchen. Reyes was still washing dishes. "Hello," Clare said, and indicated her tray. "Sorry to be adding to the pile." She unloaded her tray, taking care to put the glassware first and the plates and saucers next. She was rewarded by a flash of dark eyes. "Reyes is an interesting name. It's Spanish, isn't it? Doesn't it mean kings?"

Another flash. Clare couldn't tell if the other woman understood her or not. "My name is Clare," she said, enunciating each word slowly and distinctly. "I work at the Harvey House." She looked down at the white apron over the black dress. In spite of all her efforts the apron was somewhat the worse for the day's wear. "I guess you could tell that already." She looked up again and tapped her chest. "Clare." She pointed at Reyes. "Reyes."

The other woman's hands stilled in the dishwater. "Rrrrrreyes."

"Oh. You roll the r." She tried it, trilling out the first letter and landing hard enough on the s to make it sound like a z. "Rrrrrrrrrrrrrrrrrayezzzzzzz."

She looked up to see a slight smile on Reyes' face and grinned. "That sounded more like a bird call than it did someone's name, didn't it? I apologize. They only taught us Latin and French at school."

"They teach us many useless things at school."

"Oh! Hello, there!" Clare heard her own words and shook her head. "Could I sound more foolish? My apologies again, Reyes. Is—is English your, ah, native tongue? You talk like—" She almost said "an American" and caught herself just in time. "You speak it so well."

The look in Reyes' eyes told Clare she knew very well what Clare had been about to say. "We learned English in the mission school. The nuns were very strict."

"I was taught by Quakers myself. They were strict, too." She picked up a dish towel to start drying the stack of dishes on the sideboard. "Has Mabel gone home?"

"Yes."

"Her sister, Florence, told me of her husband's death. Horrible."

"Mm."

Ida and Elizabeth came in, chattering animatedly, with laden trays, unloaded them on the sideboard, and departed, still chattering.

Clare waited hopefully, and was rewarded.

"Mabel can find a better one."

Clare hesitated. "Yee-eees. Florence seems to think the same, more or less."

"He came here to meet with Mr. Gowan."

"Mabel's husband did?"

Reyes scrubbed viciously at something encrusted on the inside of a bowl. "Yes. Always he found the time to visit the kitchen. He says it's for food, but—"

"Did he harass you?"

Reyes snorted. "My daughter Ana. Once only." She glanced up and Clare followed her gaze to the immense knife block, no slot of which was empty. Some of the handles looked as if they would be better suited to a pickaxe. "I stopped it."

I'll bet you did, Clare thought. "I wonder why he came here. He didn't work for Mr. Gowan, he worked for the railroad."

Reyes shrugged. "Not my business. I work here to support my family back at the pueblo." She held up the bowl, one of the Fred Harvey serving bowls, and examined it, back and front. She shook her head, rinsed it, and handed it to Clare.

Clare took it and looked it over. It looked all right to her, no chips or cracks, the pattern unfaded. "Did you see something wrong with this bowl, Reyes?"

Reyes cast the bowl a disparaging glance. "It's fine for what it is."

"You... know something about bowls?"

Reyes gave Clare a pitying look that forgave her her white, eastern ignorance. "The Tewa are the world's best potters. My sister, Nicolasa, makes storage jars and cooking pots and eating bowls that are beautiful enough to make you weep. Those?" A regal wave of her hand dismissed the bowl Clare was holding. "Those are made by machine, as many as possible as fast as possible. Cheap, tough, easily replaceable. They do very well for the Harvey Houses."

Clare heard a sound behind them and looked over her shoulder to see Fred Harvey standing in the doorway. His face was a study, whether because of the discovery that Reyes spoke perfect English or because of her criticism of his crockery. Clare bit back a smile. "Yes, Mr. Harvey?"

He cleared his throat. "One last sweep should do it, I think, Miss Wadsworth."

"Of course, Mr. Harvey." Clare wiped the bowl dry and nested it on top of the five just like it with care. "It was lovely to visit with you, Reyes. I hope we meet again."

"You should visit our pueblo."

"Where is it?"

"A day by wagon from Santa Fe. I will show you our pottery, and you will be able to tell the difference." She didn't so much as look at Fred Harvey but Clare got the feeling her words were meant for him.

"Thank you for the invitation," Clare said. "One day I hope to take you up on it."

## 11

> "It's a pretty deep cut with, I'd say, a very, very sharp knife. I'd guess death occurred within thirty seconds."

### April 5, 1890

### Saturday

Harvey gave her an odd look when she came into the hall but he said only, "I believe the upstairs north wing could use a last look, Miss Wadsworth."

"Yes, Mr. Harvey."

She went quickly up the stairs, turned right, and decided to go all the way down to the end of the hall and work her way back. There was a bay window with a courting chair upholstered in light blue brocade in front of it, facing outward. She lingered for just a moment to admire the view of the red mountains darkening to black and the stars trembling into being, and then looked beneath the chair to find an empty coffee cup, a martini glass with a cigarillo stubbed out in it, and a used rubber condom.

Lovely.

She used the edge of the coffee cup to scoop the condom onto the tray and then turned the cup upside down over it with the intention of smuggling it to the kitchen for disposal in the trash. No need to traumatize Reyes or anyone else, although she suspected that the other girls would have equally disgusting stories of their own.

The dark blue velvet drapes were drawn back from the window but the holdbacks had not been fastened, from which she deduced that the couple trysting on the courting chair sometime during the at-home had drawn the curtains for privacy. She pulled the drapes back into their intended graceful folds and secured them, although there was a slight feeling of going above and beyond the call for the entire exercise.

She walked down the hall toward the stairs, holding the tray at arm's length, trying doors as she went and being quick and not necessarily quiet about it, as Mr. Clemens had been revealed to be lodging in the south wing downstairs.

Halfway down she found a door slightly ajar. It was directly across the hall from the Marie Antoinette bedroom, and she remembered it had been closed at the time of Mr. Gowan's tour and that Gowan had passed it by as if it hadn't been there.

She did not hesitate, slipping inside, the tray on her arm a ready excuse.

The door swung wider on well-oiled hinges, revealing a room lined with glass-front cabinets and filled with glass display cases. She moved to one of the cases and was astonished to see a tiara made of what looked like real gold, embellished with red, blue, and green cabochons of what might be gemstones if the metal really was gold. A small, neatly lettered card read "Royal circlet, English, found near Winchester, circa 875, possibly Alfred the Great's coronation crown."

Really. Alfred the Great's coronation crown. Tucked into a display case in the New Mexico Territory, an entire ocean and most of a continent away from where Alfred the Great was crowned. Clare felt ever so slightly skeptical.

The next case held a circlet made of continuous golden knots each an inch wide. The card here read "Gold diadem, Ptolemaic, circa 250 BC, found in Alexandria, possibly dating from the time of Ptolemy III Euergetes."

Yes, well, and here was an artifact most of a continent, a whole ocean and an entire sea away from the land that saw it made and worn.

Another case held a bejeweled scepter, unidentified. A fourth presented her with a parure of diamonds and emeralds labeled as having once belonged to Empress Marie Louise, Napoleon's wife.

The voices and movements taking place elsewhere in the house receded to a distant hum. Undeniably bemused, reluctantly enchanted, Clare drifted toward the shelves lining the walls, each filled with treasures and oddities equally rare. A pitcher less than six inches high whose ceramic body was made in the likeness of the head of a Persian prince wearing a turban with what was either glass or a real emerald in its center. A pair of polished wooden harps that stood on their own two bent legs, each with carved African heads and arched necks lined with tuning pins. If art was supposed to make you feel happy, these succeeded.

She saw next a collection of implements with a display card reading "The contents of a doctor's bag dug from the ashes of Pompeii, Italy" that included a scalpel, a pair of tweezers, and various other instruments that one could only hope had been as useful to the physician as they looked uncomfortable to the patient.

There was more, much too much more to be taken in at one glance. There seemed to her to be a preponderance of royal regalia, more circlets for head, wrist, and arm made of gold, silver, bronze, and one set that looked like a rude kind of steel, two more scepters, a solid gold torc with gold teardrop pendants dangling all the way around.

There was a large copper basin, an ovoid some three feet across. Bas-reliefs were worked into the lip and around the foot, figures too tiny to work out without a magnifying glass. The copper was so highly burnished it seemed she could almost smell the metal from inside its display case.

Ozymandias.

"Look on my works, ye mighty, and despair?" a voice said behind her.

She started and turned to see Wash Gowan in the doorway, regarding her with a quizzical expression. She met his gaze blankly for a moment, and then laughed involuntarily. "I'm sorry. I didn't realize I'd said that out loud."

"Ozymandias?" He strolled up to stand beside her. "Is that what this room looks like to you?"

She raised her eyebrows. "A threadbare glove from the past thrown down to the present?"

He shook his head. "No." He took her hand and held it between his own, looking at it. "Don't do that."

Unsettled by the touch of his hand and determined not to show it, she let her hand lie resistless in his own. "Do what?"

He raised his hand to her lips and held it there for a long moment. They felt warm and firm on her skin and it was impossible for her not to wonder what they would feel like pressed to her own. "Belittle my collection as a means of defending yourself."

He turned her hand and pressed another kiss to her palm. She could not repress a gasp. He recognized her reaction and a glint appeared in his eye.

As gently as possible she withdrew her hand from his. "I doubt anyone could belittle this collection, Mr. Gowan." She turned away so she wouldn't have to see his expression, afraid of what her own might give away. She didn't even like the man, for heaven's sake.

From behind her he said, "I'm afraid my reasons for collecting are a little more prosaic."

Surprised, she glanced back. "Prosaic?"

"The Irish have a saying about land. 'They aren't making any more of it.'" He nodded at the collection. "They aren't making any more of these, either. Their rarity makes them more valuable as time goes on, and very easy to convert into cash, if it became necessary."

"I see. A sort of savings account."

"Yes, but one with a better rate of interest than anything you'd find in a bank."

"Did you collect all the pieces yourself?"

"Or did I have someone buy them for me? With instructions to purchase the most valuable items he could find regardless of their cultural or historical or artistic value so as to enhance my reputation as a collector?"

Involuntarily she turned and caught a flash of anger in his dark eyes. She refused to be intimidated but there was no profit in alienating him entirely. "I apologize. I'm afraid I was raised to tell the truth and shame the devil."

He smoothed the anger over with a smile that felt forced. "Go ahead."

She cast a long, assessing look around the room. "Then, yes, your collection feels a little… gaudy." She turned to face him fully. "If I were only judging from its setting, I could even call it precarious."

He frowned. "I'm afraid I don't understand."

"Precarious in that an exhibit such as this in a two-year-old frontier town in a territory that isn't even yet a state, where the only law enforcement officer I've yet seen spends most of his time in a drunken stupor and where people settle their differences daily with guns in the street…" She shrugged. "I'm surprised you don't have one guard sitting outside the door and an army of them patrolling outside the window every moment of the day."

His mouth twisted up at one corner. "So noted." He looked back at the door. "Usually that door is locked." He looked back at her, his eyebrows raised.

She shrugged. "I was doing a last sweep of this wing and the door was open. I came in to check it, and I… well." She raised an eyebrow. "I guess I was diverted."

"Diverted?"

She laughed a little. "All right then, enchanted." She turned back to the copper vessel in the case. "This is magnificent. So old, and yet it could have come from the metalsmith's hands yesterday. You can almost smell the copper..."

She stiffened and inhaled deeply.

Yes. A strong, coppery smell.

"What?" Gowan stirred next to her. "What is it?"

"Clare?" She heard Florence's voice behind her at the door. "Oh my goodness! What is all this?"

"Stay where you are, Florence." Without conscious thought she had pulled out her derringer and now ensured that it was concealed beneath the edge of her apron. "Mr. Gowan, if you would please step out into the hall."

"I beg your pardon?"

She looked at him and for just a moment, just long enough for it to be felt, she let the Harvey Girl persona drop. "If you would please step out into the hall."

When he looked up at her again he appeared angry, baffled, and yet somehow accepting of her authority. He gave a curt nod and went to stand in the doorway, either accidentally or intentionally blocking Florence's view. Regardless, she stood on tiptoe to peer over his shoulder, her expression at first awed by the riches on display, and then slowly horrified at the sight of what lay beyond them.

Dark red velvet drapes hung across what proved to be an immense leaded-glass window. There was no sign to indicate its provenance but that was not her chief concern at the moment. She took a step forward and pulled the left drape to one side.

Louis Abernathy lay on the floor between drape and window, in a pool of what could only be his own blood on the floor beneath him.

She heard an intake of breath behind her. "Don't scream, Florence. Do not scream." The last thing they needed was a stampede of all the staff into this room.

A shaky breath and then Florence said, "All—all right. Clare, who is it?"

"Mr. Gowan, could you please fetch Mr. Harvey?"

"Certainly."

"The sheriff, too. He was asleep in the one of the chairs in the library earlier." She bent to touch two fingers to Abernathy's neck. The flesh was cooling and there was no pulse. Knowing it was no use she added, "And the doctor." Although Abernathy was beyond any medical attention.

Footsteps receded down the carpeted hall.

There was no one else behind the drapery and the window did not open and had not been broken. She pocketed her derringer and turned to see Florence in the doorway. Her voice was barely audible. "Clare, was that a pistol? What would you be doing with a—" She swayed, her hand going to the edge of the door.

"Oh no, no, no, no you don't." She went quickly forward to take Florence by the arm and guide her to a Windsor chair that probably dated back to the French and Indian War. She pushed Florence's head down to her knees. "Breathe, Florence. In, out. In, out. Good. Good, that's the way, good."

"I'm all right," the other girl said in a faint voice. "Truly, Clare. I'm all right now." She sat up, her face a little less white but still strained. "Was that— Who was that?"

"Don't worry about that now."

"Was it—was it Mr. Abernathy?"

Clare looked at her, a little puzzled. Other than Henrietta, none of the employees at the Montaña Roja Harvey House harbored any affection for Abernathy, and she couldn't understand what appeared to be the faint but unmistakable edge of terror in Florence's voice. "Yes—" And then she had to push Florence's head down to her knees again. "Breathe. In. Out. In. Out. That's it." She waited until the other girl was upright again. "Florence? What's wrong?"

Florence's laugh was slight and shaky. "Other than my boss dead on the floor in the next room? Nothing. Nothing at all." She looked down the hall and said with relief, "Oh thank goodness. There's Mr. Harvey."

There indeed was Mr. Harvey, who wasn't quite running but he was a step ahead of Gowan with Mr. Clemens bringing up the rear. Behind them everyone else clustered at the head of the stairs, all agog. This included Henrietta, who as near as Clare could tell looked like someone who ought to be sobbing her heart out but couldn't quite work up the necessary feeling. Florence rose to her feet and went to her side.

Clare turned to Mr. Harvey, who was standing at the door of the one-room museum. "Probably best to stay in the hall, Mr. Harvey. Until the doctor gets here."

Harvey, staring across the room at the body, looked at her. "Of course." He fell back a pace. "Of course."

He didn't looked frightened or horrified or stricken with grief. He looked angry.

No. He looked enraged.

And no wonder. Clare was more than a little peeved herself.

He looked at her. "His throat was cut?"

"Yes." She knew he had the same thought. Abernathy's throat was cut just like Harry Funston's throat had been cut on a full moon night north of Fort Union two months before.

Harvey turned to look at Gowan. "This door was locked when you gave us the tour."

"Yes."

"When did you unlock it?"

"I didn't." He gestured impatiently. "I mean, I did, once, to show Clemens my collection."

Clemens nodded confirmation.

"But I locked it again when we left."

Harvey looked at Clemens, who nodded again.

Gowan put his hand in his pocket and produced a ring of keys and held one up. "This one right here."

"You keep them with you?"

He stiffened. "They never leave my person."

"Is there a spare key?" Clare said.

"Yes."

"Where is it?"

"In the safe. In my office."

"Move the hell out of the way." The impatient voice came from behind the crowd at the top of the stairs. Sheriff Parker, looking all the better (and more sober) for his nap, shoved his way to the top of the stairs and strode down the hallway.

He nodded at Gowan. "Bob went for the doc." He looked at Harvey. "Where?"

Harvey pointed.

Clare faded into the background, eventually coming to rest against one of the few sections of wall free of adornment. She was joined a moment later by Mr. Clemens. "The joy of killing," he said, rolling one of his cigars between his fingers but not lighting it. "The joy of seeing killing done."

He was watching the cluster of people at the head of the stairs, craning their necks to see what they could see, daring one step closer, another.

She wanted to say something in defense of the people she worked with, but she couldn't because she knew he was right. Murder was always a spectator sport.

He pointed his chin at the open door. The sheriff was stooping over the body, with Harvey and Gowan watching. "Did you know him?"

He was curious. Well, of course he was; they all were. "He was the manager of the Harvey House in Montaña Roja. Louis Abernathy."

She almost said "Did you know him?" in turn, but thought better of it.

"Shot?"

"No." She didn't elaborate.

"Please let the doctor through, ladies, gents, thank you." Bob Parker appeared at the head of the stairs with Dr. Irwin in tow. The latter carried his black bag and allowed Parker to escort him to the room and inside. The sheriff followed.

"Yes, well. Not much doubt the man is dead, as no one could live through a wound like that, not even in the five seconds after it was inflicted." Irwin sighed. "But let's go through the motions."

He went down on one knee, made a perfunctory check for a pulse at wrist and, gingerly, throat, and put his ear next to Abernathy's mouth. "No pulse, not breathing. From the quantity of blood on the floor alone I think I could reliably state that he's dead." He raised Abernathy's chin slightly and winced. "There is an incision almost from ear to ear on the throat, and—" he used both hands to raise up the body and cast a quick glance along the back "—pretty safe to say the cause of death was due to blood loss from the wound. What— good god."

"What, doc?"

Clare hadn't known that the rotund, cheerful little doctor could sound so grim. "The killer did a thorough job, I'll say that for him. His head nearly fell off when I moved him. Look, you can see his spine."

A momentary silence, when Clare imagined everyone was having trouble controlling their stomach. She was.

She felt Harvey looking at her, and knew again that they were both thinking the same thing: that Harry Funston's wound had been so severe that his head had fallen off his body when the engineers lifted him into the car.

"Any idea when he got cut, doc?" The sheriff.

"Well, the body hasn't stiffened up yet." Irwin looked at the dark red pool and touched one finger to the surface. "The blood's pretty tacky. My guess is anywhere between one and three hours ago." He stood up. "It's a pretty deep cut with, I'd say, a very, very sharp knife, so I'd guess death occurred within thirty seconds." He looked at Gowan. "There is probably spatter."

Gowan nodded. "We smelled it. That's how we knew."

Oh we did, did we? Clare thought. On the other hand, the less attention drawn to herself the better. She saw Harvey turn in her direction and she looked down to avoid his gaze.

"Have you seen Gowan's museum?"

She raised her head to look at Clemens, who was still watching the tableau grouped around the body. "Yes. Mr. Gowan was showing it to me when we found the body."

"Ah. And what do you think of it?"

She said demurely, "No real lady will tell the naked truth in the presence of gentlemen."

He gave a crack of laughter, quickly muffled when people turned shocked looks on him. "What kind of Harvey Girl is this, that she may quote my own words back to me?"

"The usual kind, Mr. Clemens."

"I find myself more interested than ever in what your answer might be to my original question."

She hesitated, and he simply waited for her to fill the vacuum of his silence. She sighed. "Loot."

"Loot," he said, chewing over the word as if it had an actual taste. "Loot. As in a pirate's hoard?"

"Pirates don't buy, they steal."

"So they don't. So they don't. The crown jewels collected in the Tower of London, then." He saw her expression. "What, my dear?"

"It's just that—" she gestured "—the majority of what is in there seems to be royal regalia of various kinds."

"So it does," Clemens said, "and you would do well to remember that, my dear."

There was a murmur of voices from within the room and Bob Parker came out into the hallway and, of course, winked at her as he passed by. She heard his boots clatter on the stairs as Fred Harvey came out to address them. "I know you're all exhausted, so Mr. Parker has gone to hitch up the wagon. Gather your belongings and meet him at the front door."

"But who was it, Mr. Harvey? Who was killed?"

He hesitated and Clare looked at Florence, who was standing hand in hand with Henrietta, who looked white and shocked but in control. It wouldn't be a surprise to her, then. Good for Florence.

Harvey made up his mind. "I'm very much afraid that Mr. Abernathy was attacked sometime during this evening. He, er, did not survive." There were gasps, so evidently the word hadn't gotten entirely around. "The doctor is ascertaining the cause of death and the sheriff will investigate to find out who perpetrated this foul deed. Now." He glanced at Gowan. "I know you all share with me your sympathy for Mr. Gowan, who opened his home to the community and whose hospitality was roughly abused in so doing. However, the tragic circumstances cannot and will not obscure the fact that the event was an immense success, and that we are all grateful to have had a part in it. Thank you, Mr. Gowan." They shook hands while the staff chorused, "Thank you, Mr. Gowan."

In a low voice Mr. Clemens said, "Sympathy for Gowan but none for the victim? It is a shoddy poor thing, our civilization, full of cruelties and hypocrisies."

"But honest in this case," Clare said.

Their eyes met. "Ah. I see. There will be little grief shed over his death."

"Very little." She pushed away from the wall and held out her hand. "It was an honor to meet you, Mr. Clemens."

"What is your name, my dear, that I might return the compliment?"

She hesitated only a moment. "Clare Wadsworth, sir."

But he had noticed the hesitation. There were no flies on Mr. Clemens. "Well, Clare Wadsworth, the pleasure has been all mine." He bent over her hand and kissed it.

Mark Twain had kissed her hand.

It wasn't until they were jolting home in the wagon that Clare remembered the tray with the used condom hidden beneath the coffee cup, abandoned on the floor outside Gowan's hoard.

## 12

> "He don't ban it, exactly," she heard one of them say, "but all's one tot a day does is make you thirsty for more."

### April 6, 1890

### Sunday

Clare woke well before sunrise the following morning, which was annoying. It was Sunday, a day of rest for anyone but preachers and Harvey Girls. She tried to go back to sleep for another hour but it was hopeless so she got up and went to the lavatory, had a quick wash and came back to her room to dress, trying to be as quiet as possible. She was the only one up so far and she didn't want to be drawn into any conversations about the previous day until she got her thoughts into some kind of order. At some point Fred Harvey was going to want to discuss recent events.

She was twenty-two years old and in good health, but there was no getting around the fact that she was operating on the ragged edge of exhaustion by the end of every day. One thing she had not anticipated in this investigation was the physical labor involved, the lifting, the stooping, the speed necessary in getting food to the table before it cooled. And then there was the surprising amount of mental acuity essential to the job, remembering faces and the names to go with them, getting the correct orders in front of the correct customer and on the way to the table checking to see that the kitchen crew got them right, too. The sheer volume and variety of customers was taxing in the extreme, and the constant pressure from management to perform up to expectations was unnerving. A customer must be seated at a place setting that showed no trace of the last customer seated there, no matter if that last customer had walked out the door just as the new one was coming in. It was one thing if Fred Harvey found a stain on a tablecloth; it was another thing entirely if a customer did, and complained.

Certainly there had been very little time to think and none at all on the job, for it required all of her attention just to do it adequately, never mind well. She would never again take good service in a restaurant for granted, whether it was one of the Harvey Houses or not.

She retrieved the tiny notebook from the hidden pocket in her skirt, raised the blind and sat down in the rocking chair, the light of daybreak increasing to illuminate the squiggles of shorthand on the page so she didn't have to switch on the lamp. The derringer lodged uncomfortably between her leg and the arm of the chair so she took it out and placed it on the foot of the bed within easy reach.

But of course, for just a moment, she looked out her window, mountains transitioning from black to red on the left, high desert to the right, sky overhead with light creeping up the eastern horizon. Another cloudless day. How many did this part of the country have in its weather locker? It must rain sometime.

There was the report of a gunshot somewhere in town, far enough away that it didn't concern her. And then she wondered when the sound of gunshots had ceased to concern her. She patted her pocket and then looked at the derringer on the bed, small, black, and in the right hands deadly. She hoped that in the press of other concerns that Florence had forgotten the sight of Clare holding it.

Although it would be less difficult to explain carrying a derringer in a town like Montaña Roja, even for a woman. Maybe especially a woman. After all, she'd seen women in jeans wearing pistols strapped to their hips the same way men did and no one looked at them twice. And given the dearth of female companionship for the average local male, no woman could be blamed for being prepared to defend herself.

She frowned at the notebook.

Harry Funston and Louis Abernathy had both been murdered.

They had both been murdered by the same method. Their throats had been cut, with intent to kill expeditiously and no mistake about it.

It went beyond the bounds of credibility that the two murders weren't connected—indeed that the victims hadn't been killed by the same person.

Why this method? Why a knife to the throat on the high desert, and why a knife to the throat in the considerably more populated Gowan House?

Because, she thought, if it was done properly, it was as close to an utterly silent means of murder as anything could be.

Funston's murder had been late at night, next to a train full of sleeping passengers. The train robbers wanted to get away with their loot without any unnecessary fuss or bother. A gunshot might be as common in the American West as the wind blowing but it was loud and would have been sure to have woken someone. And that someone could have been curious enough to investigate, which would only complicate the job at hand, and trying to deal with angry, frightened civilians might lead to an increase in the body count in a way that focused more attention from the authorities. Clare had enough respect for the brains behind this operation to believe that the plan for the train robberies would have included a response to every imaginable incident.

Abernathy was murdered in the early evening, at the end of a day-long busy, crowded event. Clare thought that the doctor's estimated time of death was probably accurate, but she leaned toward the long end of that estimate rather than the short. An hour before Clare and Gowan found the body the house had for the most part emptied out and it would have been quieter, possibly too quiet to hide the sounds of the attack. Three hours before, every open room would have been filled with the conversation and laughter of hundreds of people, the volume of which increased as the bottles of alcohol emptied out. All the killer had to do was wait for the opportunity.

Go west, young man, stick a knife into any available target and you will be well paid for your blood crimes.

It would have been easy to lure Abernathy away for a look at Gowan's collection of plunder. But to do that, the killer would have to have, first, known the room existed, and second, known that Gowan kept a spare key in his safe, and its combination. Which argued that the killer must be one of Gowan's inner circle. Bob Parker? Any one of the men who regularly lunched with him at the Harvey House and presumably visited him here? But that would include Dr. Irwin and the commanding officer of Fort Union, both of whom were present at the at-home. Reyes? Mark Twain?

And maybe Gowan was lying, and he had been the one luring Abernathy to his doom and opening the door with the key from his own pocket.

And maybe the killer, not only an expert lockpick, was also an expert pickpocket, so skilled as to be capable of lifting the key from Gowan's pocket and returning it again without him being in the least aware.

Clare rolled her eyes. This was the stuff of fantasy, although she wouldn't mind betting that there were many people who would be more than happy to buy into the idea of a complete stranger infiltrating Gowan House, committing bloody murder, and leaving again unseen, unheard, and uncaught. The first thing any investigation destroyed was privacy, and Clare would bet both of her salaries that there were any number of bodies buried in the backyards of people who wanted them to stay there. In her experience, there always were.

She riffled through the pages of the notebook. The contents would have been unreadable for anyone who hadn't been force marched through a Pitman class—deciphering it herself was often a challenge—but it ensured that very few other people would be able to read her notes on the case should the notebook fall into the wrong hands. At the moment she wasn't reading in depth herself, only refreshing her memory on details, evidence, speculation she had jotted down.

She frowned and closed the notebook. What about motive?

It felt like there was more than enough to go around. Too much, in fact.

It was probable that Harry Funston had conspired to help rob the Atchison, Topeka and Santa Fe Railroad not once but four times over the past year. It also seemed from the cursory look she'd had at the Montaña Roja's books that the robbers had been targeting mostly comestibles bound for Harvey Houses in the New Mexico Territory.

She might not be able to prove it—yet—but she was certain in her own mind that Abernathy and Funston had been testing the waters for at least a year prior to the first train robbery and probably since the Montaña Roja Harvey House opened, manifesting in the theft of stores from the Harvey House itself.

They must have resold them, she thought. To whom? She remembered the overheard conversation about the price of beans. That rancher would not have turned down a deal on a discounted case of canned beans and he wouldn't have inquired too closely into where it came from. Farmers, miners, lumbermen, the poor neighborhood south of the tracks. The difficulty wouldn't have been in turning over the merchandise; the difficulty would have been coming up with enough supply to meet demand.

The fact that both men were dead, both murdered, both in the same manner, only confirmed her suspicion that their fellow thieves were cleaning up after themselves. Leaving no witnesses behind left only the ledgers, and with both Abernathy and Funston unable to testify as to their veracity meant the blame would stop with them.

But she had told Fred Harvey on Thursday night that whoever was or had been organizing the robberies had brains, resources, and manpower.

Again, she thought of the men around Gowan's table, and of Gowan himself. Gowan had all the money, hired support, and influence needed to orchestrate the thefts, but for the life of her, she couldn't imagine Gowan risking what he already had in robbing trains to get more of what he already had. His people were well paid, well fed, well housed, and most seemed on the face of it loyal enough to stay employed, so that let off Bob Parker, too, at least provisionally.

Half the time the sheriff was incompetent from drink and it was difficult to imagine him masterminding an operation of this magnitude.

While Clare was well aware of the many and juicy opportunities for graft in the United States Army, to her knowledge that kind of thing more often occurred at a lower level of command, among the enlisted men or junior officers. Lieutenant Colonel Benteen would be risking a great deal: dismissal, disgrace, prosecution, incarceration. A lifetime at Leavenworth was a pretty grim prospect. He'd brought his wife and two children to dinner at the Harvey House, coming down from Fort Union on the train one Saturday and returning on Sunday. His wife was lovely in form and manner, his children well-behaved, and he himself seemed pleased with them and his life in general. She had heard no rumors to his discredit from other soldiers from the fort, who deemed him strict but fair. The only complaints were about the daily weapons drills and his insistence on his men learning to ride and care for their horses, and a few bitter remarks about the iron grip he maintained on alcohol. "He don't ban it, exactly," she had heard one of them say, "but all's one tot a day does is make you thirsty for more."

She doubted that any of Benteen's superiors in the Department of War would take issue with any of his orders of the day.

However, there was that conversation, if you could call it that, with the grandee at Gowan's at-home. Too few and not enough of what?

She kept him on the list but at the bottom, one up from Bob Parker.

The grandee was one Gabriel Romero Rubio y Castelló, allegedly a relation of Porfirio Díaz's wife, and here, context would be everything. She reviewed what information she knew about the country south of the border. Six years before, Díaz had arranged for the Mexican constitution to be altered so as to allow the president to run for re-election for life. He had subsequently rolled out the welcome mat for American industrialists to cross the border at will, there to start and run manufacturing and resource extraction businesses. The proceeds of those businesses, already large, were made larger when they were required to pay no taxes by the Mexican government. They were of course somewhat diminished when a portion found its way into the pockets of Díaz and, presumably, his family. Again, on the face of it

Clare could see no motive for someone of Rubio y Castelló's closeness to power and presumed share of kickbacks to act against his own interests. Unless, of course, he wanted more.

Which could also apply to Gowan, she thought.

She put Rubio y Castelló's name at the middle of the list, ready to move up or down depending on information received in future.

Walter Dabney, the Indian agent, she put at the top of the list, in part because she found his personal manner so repellant but mainly because the reputation of Indian Agents was so uniformly bad. A week didn't pass without some story in the newspapers about an Indian agent getting caught with his hand in the federal till, subverting funds to his own benefit while shorting the tribes it was his sworn duty to feed, clothe, house, and educate. The cringing, obsequious Dabney looked one invitation away from jumping feet first into any crooked scheme that would work to his benefit, and while Clare was familiar with the old adage about beauty and the eye of the beholder, she took some satisfaction in putting him at the top of the list.

Which task she admitted was made easier by the fact that there was plenty of room there, but Chessie in Santa Fe would be pleased.

Dudley Platt, he of the Montaña Roja Trust and Savings Bank and the town magistrate, looked the most upright of the lot. One could learn a lot about someone by waiting on them at table, and the banker was a mild-mannered, pleasant fellow who treated friends and staff alike with the same courtesy. He didn't speak often but she noticed that when he did the others stopped to listen, including Gowan.

She put him in the middle, below Rubio y Castelló.

She closed her eyes and leaned her head back against the chair and rocked.

The fact was there was only one name on the list with the qualities she had told Fred Harvey were necessary: brains, resources, and manpower, and that was George Washington "Wash" Gowan.

She could only imagine Fred Harvey's reaction if she told him her chief suspect in robbery and murder was his business partner, Wash Gowan.

She sighed.

The much-anticipated letter from Robert Pinkerton had come on the day before Fred Harvey arrived and had provided little new information. The witnesses interviewed after the first three train robberies had, yes, heard another engine. A quick and probably cursory investigation had revealed nothing to detract from Gowan or his cronies. Gowan had cut corners, as Robert put it, but then who among successful businessmen out there hadn't? Most of them hadn't stopped at cutting corners, either. One of the reasons Clare was happy to work undercover was because she never had to explain the Pinkerton Detective Agency's behavior in the Great Railroad Strike of 1877.

There was movement outside her window and she looked up to see a small herd of pronghorn antelope nosing around a thick stand of sagebrush that lined the south side of the tracks. This herd was closer than the one she had seen from the train and she could see even more clearly how beautiful they were, with delicately curved horns, white bellies and rumps, and golden brown backs.

Something else you wouldn't see on Michigan Avenue in Chicago.

The herd scattered suddenly, bounding off in different directions, seconds ahead of a mountain lion which burst out of the sagebrush. It landed on the back of one of the adults too slow to leap away, knocking it down and biting through its neck. Clare imagined hearing its spine break between those powerful jaws. The antelope gave one futile kick and died.

Clare found herself standing with her nose pressed to the window as that magnificent beast dragged his kill into the underbrush. A moment later and both herd, kill, and cat had vanished as if they had never been there. The only evidence of their presence was the rapid beating of her heart and the trembling of her knees.

Violent death was everywhere she looked in this territory. Harry Funston. Louis Abernathy. Georgie gunning down Johnny in a drunken rage. The mountain lion and the antelope. Nature red in tooth and claw.

What was it Mr. Clemens had said the night before? *The joy of killing. The joy of seeing killing done.* If Mr. Darwin was right, it was the survival of the fittest. The man who drew first and fastest versus the man who couldn't get his weapon out of the holster. The slowest antelope falling victim in the attack, leaving the faster ones to escape and breed faster offspring.

Funston and Abernathy, tools to be discarded when they were no longer useful.

At least the cougar killed to eat. Survival was its motivation, not enrichment.

She subsided back into the rocking chair. The quiver of sagebrush concealing the lion and its breakfast subsided.

Come at it from another angle. What if both murders were personal? What if they had nothing to do with the train robberies?

Florence didn't like her brother-in-law because he was "too grabby." He'd made advances to Reyes' daughter Juanita. What if Funston made a habit of forcing his attentions on women? What if he'd been grabbing at women up and down the high iron? What if one of them— better, what if one of their husbands had taken exception, had been traveling on the Red Mountain Express that night, had seen an opportunity and taken it?

What if Mabel was aware of his philandering? Could she have somehow followed him up on the train and killed him on the way down?

But then again, while she might have been a betrayed wife, she was also a mother. She might be angry enough to kill, but would she risk orphaning her children?

Suddenly she remembered the expression on Mabel's face when she looked up to see Abernathy in the doorway. For just a moment it had looked like pure hatred.

She remembered the knife block in the kitchen, one of every shape and size imaginable. Mabel was a cook, a chef. She knew how to use a knife.

Had she done so not once, but twice?

And then, reluctantly, Clare came to Henrietta.

*I thought he loved me. He said he did, and I believed him.*

Of course Henrietta had, because she had wanted to so badly. Abernathy had only told her what he knew she wanted to hear to get what he wanted, what a thousand, million other men had told another thousand, million women to get what they wanted. It was the oldest story, second only to *The woman tempted me and I ate it.*

If not a cook herself, Henrietta would have easy access to any knife she chose in the kitchen. Abernathy would be unsuspecting, because he wouldn't anticipate anything more than harsh words and resentment from any of his women, probably because he'd seen nothing else.

And wasn't that a poor reflection on womankind as a whole, Clare thought. Not that she wanted her sex to go around exacting a life for every instance of what was at least in part their own bad judgement, but...

*I did everything he asked of me, even...*

Clare sat bolt upright in the rocking chair, for the first time since her arrival staring at the landscape outside her window without appreciation. It was by now flooded with sunshine.

*I did everything he asked of me, even...*

Even? Even what?

Suppose Henrietta was Abernathy's dupe for more than sex?

Elizabeth was the oldest of Montaña Roja's Harvey Girls but Henrietta had worked there from the day it opened.

So had Abernathy, and by the House's own books Clare could see that he had begun stealing almost as soon as the first trainload of hungry passengers was served their lunch.

Suppose Henrietta had been the first to catch him at it?

A door banged in the hallway and she jumped. She heard Elizabeth say with disgust, "Oh, look, someone didn't flush. Disgusting."

"Flush it, then, Elizabeth." Henrietta. "And maybe wipe off the seat."

Clare got up and immediately noticed the lack of the familiar weight in her pocket. She looked around and found her pistol sitting on the foot of her bed where she'd placed it when she sat down. She picked it up and from long habit pulled the hammer back to the half-cock position to check the cap, and let it down carefully again.

It was the same make and model of weapon with which President Abraham Lincoln had been killed on that awful night in Ford's Theater. Clare wouldn't be born for another three years but it was an event that had helped build the world she lived in and both the Quakers at the Quaker school and her teachers at Vassar had made sure she knew it. It wasn't difficult, as Lincoln had written some of the finest words in the history of the nation, words that stood on the same level and in some instances higher than anything written by the Founding Fathers.

She only wished he'd included women in the Emancipation Proclamation. For saying so out loud in sixth grade she had been called irreverent and disrespectful and was condemned to sit on a high stool with a dunce cap on her head for the rest of the class period. Worse, she was required to write a five-hundred-word essay on the life of the sixteenth president. By then she understood her Quaker teachers' adoration of Lincoln, but she wondered how many of them knew that Lincoln had issued the Emancipation Proclamation in the hope that it would encourage slaves to revolt against the Confederacy, and that he had originally encouraged the notion of shipping the enslaved back to Africa. She did not include either item in her essay, which was undoubtedly why she graduated from Quaker school with a passing grade in American History.

The man had been dead now for twenty-five years to the month, and still his shade lingered across the land. It was impossible not to wonder what the country would have looked like if he had survived his second term.

What she had told Harvey was true; the Pinkertons hadn't been on duty that night. She also wondered what had happened to the Washington D.C. police officer who was supposed to have been on guard outside the door to Lincoln's box. Stories abounded as to where he had been instead, from sitting in the audience watching the performance to drinking in the saloon next door. What was not in dispute was that he hadn't been sitting outside Lincoln's box. If he had been, Booth wouldn't have gotten inside, Philadelphia derringer in one hand and knife in the other, and…

She sat down suddenly on her bed.

Parker.

Fred Parker.

John Parker.

She drew in a deep breath and let it out slowly.

John Frederick Parker.

That was the name of the Washington D.C. police officer.

For reasons best known to the Washington D.C. Police Department, Parker hadn't been fired or even disciplined for his dereliction of duty at Ford's Theater. He was fired in 1868, for sleeping on the job. Which every Pinkerton agent who knew the story instantly translated to "passed out while drunk on duty."

If Bob Parker's Uncle Fred and John Frederick Parker were one and the same, she wondered what he was doing in

New Mexico Territory. Perhaps it was the only one where his employers didn't care if he was drunk on duty.

Which begged the question, why didn't they care?

He had danced so beautifully at the Lightfoot that evening, never losing his balance, never off the beat, never missing a step, able to converse sensibly while never bumping into any of the other couples.

There was a knock at her door. "Clare?"

"Yes, I'm awake, Florence, thank you. I'll be right down."

She became aware that she was still holding the derringer. It was designed for close work, but she had hit her target from twenty-five feet. Well, once. And it had been a calm day, too, and the target stationary. She didn't know that she could do it again. When she had to shoot she made sure she was a lot closer than that.

So had John Wilkes Booth.

The paper of extra cartridges was still in her pocket. She replaced the notebook and the derringer and smoothed her apron.

Her next task was to arrange to speak to Henrietta privately.

Her mental and physical exhaustion was replaced by a wave of exhilaration, familiar to her from previous cases. She had experienced it that last day at Bienville, when she knew Calhoun was going to break, and she felt it now.

Henrietta could hold the key to everything and blow this case wide open.

## 13

"Like I told you, darlin'. We're all killers here."

### April 6, 1890

#### Sunday

Easier said than done because everyone in Montaña Roja who hadn't attended Gowan's at-home the day before overwhelmed the restaurant that Sunday and it was clear they weren't there only to eat. Clare found at least half of her time taken up by customers who wanted to know a minute-by-minute recounting of yesterday's events, as well as a detailed description of Gowan House, and was it true there was a fortune in gold in one of the rooms?

And oh yes, they supposed they'd order a meal while they were there, the luncheon special was fine, but wasn't Miss—what was it, again—Dodsworth or Woolsworth or Waddleton—hadn't she been serving at Gowan House the day before? Someone said there had been a murder, imagine! Someone else said Mark Twain had been there. Someone else said Mark Twain had been killed. Was that true? No? The speaker tried not to sound too disappointed.

No table emptied out that wasn't immediately refilled by entire families or eight strangers, whoever elbowed their way into them first. People around the counter just stayed where they were, anchoring their seats with continuous cups of coffee and pieces of pie. Chef had to put one of the kitchen staff on permanent fetch and carry between restaurant and warehouse lest stores run out, and Fred Harvey himself sent one of the stewards to the telegraph office to dit-dah a frantic plea up the high iron to double the next day's order of coffee beans.

"Here's hoping we don't run out before the noon train," Clare heard Chef say before lunch had even begun.

By early evening, when people who had come for lunch were staying over for dinner, Elizabeth said with feeling, "This makes yesterday look like a picnic."

There were no split shifts that day and at nine p.m. that night Clare wiped down her last table and staggered upstairs, having been on her feet for eleven hours straight.

On Monday Fred Harvey departed on the Red Mountain Express southbound, making a point of saying in Clare's hearing that he would be back through in a few days. The Sunday Niagara of customers had slowed to a mere flood. On Tuesday the river had returned to within its banks. That night the steward Fred Harvey had named temporary manager decreed the split shift back for Wednesday and Thursday, the shifts divided among the staff.

Henrietta got Wednesday afternoon off. So did Clare.

"Oh lord," Clare said, stretching. "I could use some fresh air and exercise. Would you like to go for a walk?"

Henrietta, who had shadows beneath her eyes, shook her head. "I'm sorry, I'm just exhausted. All I want to do is lie down. Maybe another day."

"I quite understand. Have a good nap."

Clare understood less when, coming out of the lavatory, she caught a glimpse of Henrietta going out the back door. Clare snatched her hat and jacket from her room and went down the inside stairs and out through the kitchen. Chef blushed when she smiled at him and used the potato masher to try to turn the ham. Beauty might be only skin deep but it was on occasion very useful, as ordinarily Chef did not care for through traffic in his kitchen.

She emerged in the alley and looked left to see the hem of Henrietta's skirt whisk around the corner. The other woman crossed the avenue, walked three blocks and turned left at the first corner. Clare followed from a discreet distance, until Henrietta went into the same coffeehouse to which Bat Masterson had escorted Clare.

She found a store window across the street that gave her an excellent reflection of the coffeehouse. Henrietta had taken a seat next to the window.

Five minutes later she was joined by Bob Parker, who offered his hand to help her up from her chair, and guided her to a table that did not look directly onto the street.

It was something Bat might do.

"What so interesting, sweetheart?"

She was startled, and looked around to see Bat Masterson standing next to her with a quizzical expression on his face, dressed with his usual bespoke elegance. She looked back at the shop window and realized it held a display of pipes and cigars.

"Are you thinking of taking up smoking?"

She regained her composure and said calmly, "Just admiring the pipes. What exactly is meerschaum, anyway?"

"Not a pipe smoker myself, but I think it's some kind of stone. I'm told it floats."

She was momentarily diverted. "Stone that floats? Really?"

He shrugged.

"Look at the one carved like an old man with a beard."

"Zeus."

"How can you tell?"

"The stem is a lightning bolt."

Clare hadn't noticed. To the right of their reflection in the window she could see Henrietta's back. She shifted a little for a better look.

"Oh." She met Bat's eyes in the window. "I see."

"She's involved with the case."

"Oh. Oh, I see." His grin flashed out. "I thought you were following..." he hesitated, "Parker." She rolled her eyes and he chuckled. "Who is she?"

"Henrietta Major. She works at the Harvey House."

"Aha. Well placed to be involved."

"Yes." She sighed.

"But you don't want her to be. Yeah. That's never fun. Well." He offered his arm.

"What?"

He jerked his head at the coffeehouse. "Let's go in and see what happens."

It had been in fact just what she had been about to do, but it would be better if she went in accompanied. They would look like a courting couple, as Henrietta Major and Bob

Parker did, as did the two other couples in the coffeehouse. Safety in numbers.

She put her hand through his arm and he waited until a Chinaman pulling a two-wheeled cart full of bolts of cloth rumbled by before leading her across the street and in the door.

They paused for a moment, blinking, as if allowing their eyes to become adjusted to the light. "There's a table over here, sweetheart," Bat said in a voice that said he knew he was walking in with the prettiest woman in Montaña Roja on his arm and didn't care who heard it. He led her to the empty table on the opposite side of the room from Henrietta and Bob Parker. Henrietta didn't turn around but Bob winked at Clare.

The young waitress who had waited on them before was at their table before they had taken their seats. "What will you have, sir?" she said adoringly.

He smiled at her. She might have quivered. "Just coffee and a plate full of those little cakes, Ethel."

"Right away, sir." Although she did take an extra moment or two to take in the view.

Clare raised an eyebrow. "Ethel?"

Bat was unperturbed. "Been back a few times. Best coffee in town." He picked up her hand and played with her fingers. "How involved?"

She fluttered her eyelashes and replied in the same low voice. "I don't know, but she was carrying on with Louis Abernathy."

"Ah. The man who was killed at Wash Gowan's on Saturday."

"Yes. He'd been stealing from the Harvey House since he began work there, and I'm certain that he was part of the gang that held up those trains and killed Harry Funston."

"Can you prove it?"

"No."

Ethel bustled up with a tray and Bat let go of Clare's hand and sat back. She poured Bat's coffee and forgot Clare had a cup. When she left, reluctantly, casting a languishing backward glance that caused her to collide with another table, Bat filled Clare's cup and served her a cake. She took a sip of the coffee. He was right. It was the best in town, not excluding the Harvey House, although she'd never tell Fred Harvey so.

"And now he's dead."

"Yes." Even to her own ears Clare sounded disgruntled.

Parker passed something to Henrietta beneath the table. She weighed it in her hand and even though what she said was largely inaudible Clare could hear the anger in her tone.

"You know they'll put all the blame on him and Funston. The best scapegoat is always the dead one." Bat raised his cup in a toast. "And here they have two."

Clare couldn't deny it. He wasn't wrong.

"So." He set his cup back down. "You're all done here, then. You could go back to Chicago, tell the B's it's all tied up. We could collect our bonus and meet up in New York City." He waggled his eyebrows. "Have a wild weekend."

She gave him a look. "There is just no way that Abernathy and Funston pulled off those train robberies all by themselves. I told Harvey, they didn't have the manpower or the resources or the brains. They were small fry." She leaned forward. "And they didn't kill each other, and they didn't kill themselves. And we haven't recovered any of the stolen goods so we haven't earned a bonus. Yet."

He started to say something and was interrupted by the sound of rising voices. Henrietta was speaking at increasing volume. Parker patted her hand and she slapped it away and jumped to her feet. She whipped around and saw Clare and for a moment froze into immobility.

"Henrietta!" Clare raised a hand in a friendly wave. "I didn't see you there! Come join us!"

Henrietta raised a hand to her mouth and ran out. The bell over the door jangled discordantly at such rough usage.

Parker waited until people stopped staring to get to his feet. He sauntered over to their table.

"Lover's quarrel?" Bat said in a bland voice.

Parker snorted. "Not likely." He looked down at Clare. "You want to be careful, darlin', keeping company with this one."

"You should talk," Bat said. It didn't sound like a joke.

Parker didn't take it like one, either. Ignoring Bat, he said, "Miss Wadsworth. A pleasure to see you, anytime, anywhere."

He made it sound less like flirtation and more like a threat. She met his eyes without flinching.

He nodded as if her behavior confirmed some inner suspicion and touched the edge of his bowler. The bell jangled behind him, a discreet single chime this time.

"No point in talking to her, Clare," Bat said as she made to rise to her feet. "Even if she does talk, she won't know anything."

Clare looked after Bob Parker, and thought Henrietta might already have told her everything Clare needed to know. "But I can still ask." She lowered her chin and looked at him from beneath her lashes. "And I will."

"You're a glutton for punishment, sweetheart," he said. He walked out with her and in the street took her hand and kissed it. "Must be why the B's set such store by you."

She stared at him. "What?" She gave a short laugh. "No, they don't."

He grinned, his teeth white against his perfectly trimmed mustache. "Well, hell, sweetheart. They give you all the plum jobs." He kissed her cheek, chucked her under the chin, and sauntered off.

She headed for the biggest livery stable in town, the one closest to the station, and hired a horse and buggy. The time by the station clock was two p.m.; she was due back neat, clean, and dressed in her uniform ready to work by five. She snapped the reins and the elderly gelding between the shafts woke up, snorted, and moved off. When they got out of town she shook him into a trot. He put his ears back but complied.

Clare much preferred riding to driving and spared a thought to mourn the fact that her riding gear was in Chicago. On the other hand, once the gelding got started he didn't laze about and twenty minutes later she was making the turn for Gowan House. The scenery on the way in was even more spectacular than it had been on Saturday, partly because the buggy was much better sprung than the buckboard but mostly because she didn't have to fight anyone else for the view. She slowed the gelding to a walk and took in the acres dotted with cattle and this time saw a fenced area containing a small herd of sheep, each trailed by one, two, and three lambs. It seemed Gowan could read a return on investment as well as that anonymous rancher on Saturday, and that he, too, wasn't one to be held hostage to the Cattlemen's Association.

She pulled back on the reins and the gelding stopped, and then ambled on over to the side of the road to crop at the grass. The range of red mountains marched north and south, the tallest ones still capped with snow. Even in just four days, the cottonwoods had doubled in size, leafing out riotously in clouds of new green. They lined the course of the creek that wandered across Gowan's acres, burbling and chuckling, a delightful sound. In the distance she saw someone on a horse, who raised his hat in salute. The air was fresh and sweet with the scent of sage.

The entire West smelled like an herb garden. So long as you were upwind of the livestock.

Somewhere ahead the road ended in Gowan's very nearly palatial estate, the monument he had chosen to build to his own success. It was nothing more or less than anyone else of his financial status had done when he reached a certain level of income and started looking around for ways to enjoy it.

Clare had to lie every day, to everyone, in her job. Her most inflexible rule was that the one person she could not lie to was herself.

Everything she had said to Gowan that evening in the museum room had been deliberately designed to provoke a reaction that might reveal a little more of the man, so that she might come to some evaluation of his character. Was he the villain of this piece?

There was absolutely no doubt in her mind that Gowan had sidestepped every ordinance, law, regulation, and statute that got in his way. *The New York Times* had dubbed them "robber barons" and the name was apt because it was the truth: Laws were something other people obeyed, not them.

Not that she was in any position to throw stones. She worked for an organization notorious for renting itself out as hired muscle for businessmen, because businessmen were the ones with the money. If their workers challenged them with a strike the Pinkerton Detective Agency hired on to break it, by any means necessary. It didn't matter if the workers were striking for working conditions that wouldn't kill them on the job or better pay so they could feed their families or minimal sanitation so they didn't die of cholera by the thousands. Be the cause ever so just, it wasn't the Pink's business to fight for the right. They fought for the dollar, and their employees fought for their paychecks, Clare included.

She took another long look at the scene spread out before her like a visual feast, and clicked to the gelding to start him back down the road.

The house was every bit as gaudily impractical as it had been the first time she'd seen it but this time at least she wasn't quite so surprised.

Reyes opened the door at her knock.

"Hello again."

A faint smile, which Clare took as a good sign. "May I see Mabel?"

Reyes shook her head. "She's not here."

"Oh." Clare bit her lip. "Her sister, Florence—remember Florence from Saturday?—couldn't get off work this afternoon. She asked me to check in on her."

"Mr. Gowan is away. She has those days off."

"Is she home?"

Reyes shrugged.

"Where does she live?"

Reyes gestured to her left. "Around the house that way, past the barn and the bunkhouse. Hers is the first house on the right."

The road through the ranch buildings ended in a circle of clapboard homes. They were small and painted a painfully bright white, each with a tiny front porch, glass sash windows and wooden shingles. Each had an outhouse out the back door and there was a well beneath a windmill in the center of the circle. Not exactly up to the standard of modern conveniences as could be found in Gowan's own home but not as bad as hauling water from the river, from here half a mile away.

Behind the small white picket fence that surrounded the first house, three children played kickball. The big leather ball was taller than the youngest child but he toddled after it fearlessly, laughing. His older brother and sister were taking care to include him in the game, not kicking the ball too hard or too far out of his way.

Clare pulled up outside the gate and got down. "Hello," she said. "My name's Clare. I'm a friend of your Aunt Florence. Is your mother home?"

The girl, the tallest and eldest, ran to the front door. There was a cowbell hanging next to it with a bit of twine dangling down from the clapper. "Mama! Mama! There's someone here who knows Auntie Flo!"

Mabel appeared in the doorway, drying her hands on her apron. "Clare! How nice to see you again. Come in, come in. Come on back to the kitchen. I'm baking cookies. Excuse me a moment." She took a towel and opened the oven door, extracting a tray.

Clare closed her eyes and inhaled. "It smells like next door to heaven in here."

Mabel laughed. "It's only my mother's old recipe for jumbles. Lily, you can take one each out to the boys and one for yourself."

"May we go down to the river, Mama?"

Mabel gave her daughter a stern look. "Yes, if you promise to watch out for snakes, and don't let Walter go anywhere near the prairie dog town."

"I promise, Mama." Lily vanished out the door and Clare heard a stampede of feet and the swing of the gate.

Mabel went to the door. "And no going in deeper than your ankles, any of you!"

"We promise, Mama!"

Mabel came back into the kitchen.

Clare smiled. "Does Walter like prairie dogs?"

"Unfortunately, but the rattlers like to hide down the prairie dog holes."

"I saw a mountain lion take a pronghorn Sunday morning. From the window of my room."

Mabel shook her head. "I don't worry about the cats. They've got plenty of natural forage this time of year. Sit down, I was just about to make some coffee."

"Ought to go well with those cookies."

"I should hope so." Soon they were both seated at the table with coffee and a plate of round cookies baked a beautiful golden brown. "These are marvelous," Clare said. "So buttery."

"My mother was famous for them, and her grandmother before that. The old family recipes are always the best."

"I'll tell Florence. She'll be jealous."

"She can make them as well as I can."

Clare raised her eyebrows. "I'm afraid the Harvey House isn't that kind of kitchen. Chef is very particular after who does what within his realm."

"I can imagine. Was Florence working today?"

"Yes. The last three days have been twelve-hour days, and today they finally gave two of us split shifts so we could have an afternoon off. I expect Florence will have the afternoon off tomorrow."

"Tell her Mr. Gowan won't be back until the day after tomorrow and to come out if she can."

"I will." Clare put down her coffee cup and looked around. "This is a lovely little house. So fresh and clean and new."

"Let me give you the tour."

The parlor to the right of the door was sparsely furnished but immaculate. The kitchen was the same, holding a wooden table covered with a red gingham cloth that matched the curtains on the window, four chairs, a stove, a counter with a sink, and cupboards above and below. A tiny pantry was visible through a barely open door, and another door led out the back. The upstairs held three bedrooms, each with its own bed and the largest one with a dresser.

"A lovely little house," Clare said again when they were back at the kitchen table.

"It is, isn't it?" Mabel said, trying not to look too proud. "It's the perfect size for me and the children, and not too much for me to handle, between the children and the job. Reyes' daughter Juanita has been a godsend, and the children really like her." She chuckled. "She's teaching Lily to make tortillas." She sighed. "Mr. Gowan has been so good to us."

"You're pretty good for Mr. Gowan from what I saw last Saturday."

"You're very kind." Mabel's smile faded. "I just wish the day hadn't ended on such a dreadful note."

"You were already gone when it happened, I think."

"I was, thank heaven." Mabel shook her head. "It's been so peaceful out here. Until now."

"The cowboys—"

Mabel shook her head. "Bob—Bob Parker, that is, Mr. Gowan's foreman—told them before…" she hesitated, "well, before I moved out here, that there was to be no foolishness and that anyone who tried any would be fired." She nodded at the front door and Clare swiveled in her chair to look. "He put that bell up outside the door with his own two hands and told me to ring it loud and long if there was any kind of trouble I couldn't handle, and to tell the children the same. And in case there was he put that scattergun up over the door and made sure I knew how to use it." She shook her head and looked indulgent. "Farmer's daughter. Of course I know how to use it."

"Of course." Clare was no farmer's daughter but she knew how to use one, too. "It must be a comfort to you."

"Well." Mabel got up to refill their cups. "I've only had to use it once." She sat down again. "And that one time, it wasn't a cowboy."

Clare raised her eyebrows.

Mabel scowled. "Abernathy. Two days after I moved in, can you believe it? Harry hadn't been dead a full month."

"Did he—"

Mabel gave a grim nod. "He tried. But I grabbed the scattergun and showed him that I'd pulled back the slide lock. I told him the next time I'd shoot him if he ever set foot on the property. He must have believed me, because he left and he never came back."

"I'm not surprised." Clare nodded when Mabel looked at her. "Oh yes. I caught him with one of the girls." She held up her hand. "No, no, not Florence. One of the others."

Mabel relaxed again. "Which one?"

Clare pressed her lips together and shook her head.

"Not Elizabeth. She's older, more experienced, and focused more on unionizing the workforce than she is men. Ida? No, she wouldn't, she was raised in a very strict family."

Mabel sighed. "Of course. Henrietta."

Clare allowed herself to look surprised. "How did you know?"

"Florence has brought all the girls here at one time or another. Henrietta..." Mabel paused. "Well, let's just say that there is a girl who is always looking for the shortcut."

"She's a good worker."

"I don't doubt it, but..." Again, Mabel hesitated. "She fell in love with this house. She couldn't stop exclaiming over every little thing." She shook her head. "I mean, there she is, a Harvey Girl, living and working in a building with hot and cold running water and a flush toilet, all expenses paid and a salary besides, only herself to support." She looked around the kitchen. "And she was envious of my having this house."

She drank the rest of her coffee and set the thick white teacup down as if it were the finest of all the delicate porcelain cups on display in the kitchen cabinet at Gowan House. She looked soberly at Clare.

"I think Abernathy would have looked like a shortcut to Henrietta."

## 14

"I saw you pass that note to Mr. Harvey."

### April 9, 1890

#### Wednesday

Mabel rang the cowbell vigorously to call the children home as Clare climbed into the buggy and snapped the reins to wake the gelding from his nap. She paused, watching as the children came tumbling out of the cottonwoods, the baby riding on his brother's back, the sunlight turning their faces to pure gold. She wondered if Henrietta had seen them like that, and if it had been just more salt in the wound of Mabel having everything Henrietta wanted.

She clicked at the horse and walked him down the lane. The stable was opposite the barn and as she turned the corner of the barn, she beheld Bob Parker talking to a cowboy in chaps on a horse leading two others. "Got your bedroll? Cold on the high prairie at night."

"I do, boss, and food and water."

"Counting on you."

"You can, boss."

Parker spotted her and waved the cowboy on. The young murderer kicked his mount into a trot. He smiled shyly at Clare and raised his hat with the same hand that was holding the leading reins of the two horses. He lost his grip on the reins and, with an oath, Parker jumped forward to snatch them up and hand them back to the red-faced cowboy, who mumbled an apology and kicked savagely at his horse. His horse took exception and nearly bucked him off. He got him under control again and headed out at a run, not looking behind him.

Parker did a quick step worthy of the Lightfoot Dance Parlor and forced Clare to rein in. He walked forward to stand next to the buggy. "Darlin', you are just every damn where, now aren't you."

"I could say the same about you, Bob."

"What are you doing around these parts, darlin'? Ol' Wash ain't around."

She gave him a cool look. "Not that it is any of your business, sir, but I was visiting Mrs. Funston."

"Ah. Nice woman." And then he spoiled it by adding, "Nice-looking woman, too."

"I'm sure she'd be pleased to hear you say so, sir."

He shivered. "Brr. Did a cold wind just blow down outta the north?"

She looked away to hide her smile.

"That's better. You headed back to town? Mind if I hitch a ride?" He climbed in to sit next to her without waiting for an answer.

"I," she said, emphasizing the word, "am indeed heading back to town, where I am already late for work."

"Now just suppose—" he put his arm along the back of the seat "—just suppose we didn't go back to town. It's a lovely afternoon and working on being an even more lovely evening. I know a little place downriver, prettiest sight for a picnic you ever saw. I could raid the kitchen and we could watch the moon come up over the desert and tell each other all our secrets."

She had to admit it didn't sound like a terrible idea. She shook the gelding back into a trot. "As I said, Mr. Parker, I am already late for work."

He heaved a sad, sad sigh. "The perils of the working girl. And the perils of the man trying to woo her."

She raised an eyebrow at him.

He burst out laughing. It was a good laugh, full, robust, infectious. It was hard not to join in. "Ain't no flies on you, darlin'. You are much older than you look."

She widened her eyes. "That I am, Mr. Parker. How astute of you to notice."

"Yeah, that's me, astute as all get out."

"How long have you been working for Mr. Gowan?"

He blinked. "How'd we get from me trying to woo you to me working for ol' Wash?"

"You don't say much about yourself. I'm curious."

"You don't say anything at all about yourself, and so am I curious."

"All right. Answer my question and I'll answer one of yours."

"This oughta be fun." He settled back against the seat. "Been working for ol' Wash over a year now. My turn.

Where you from, darlin'? 'Cause I know it ain't anywhere from the Mississippi west."

"You're right about that, Mr. Parker. I was born in Saratoga, New York. And you?"

"Utah."

She looked at him in surprise. "You're a Mormon?"

"Uh-uh, I get another question first. What did you do before you were a Harvey Girl?"

"I lived at home with my parents."

"I was born a Mormon. Got a decent education out of it but nothing much else stuck. Mormons are hell on education. Why'd you leave Saratoga and come all the way out west?"

"My parents died and I had to support myself. Being a Harvey Girl was the best paying job I could find."

"Other girls get married."

"This girl might, too, some day. What have you been doing since Utah?"

"This and that. Some ranching, some herding. Worked for a butcher for a while, how I got my nickname."

"Butch. I remember, Mr. Masterson said—"

He pounced. "Yes. Now tell me, darlin', how it is you know Bat Masterson of all people?"

"We met in Kansas City, while I was in training," she said, lying impeccably like the good Pinkerton agent she was. "He took a fancy, not unlike yourself, Mr. Parker. How did you come to meet Mr. Gowan?"

"I was in Colorado, looking for a job. Ol' Wash was in town on business and passed the word he was looking for someone who knew how to ride herd on men and cattle. I went to see him and he hired me. Did Bat follow you down here?"

She gave a laugh that was both spontaneous and genuine. "You'd have to ask him, but I doubt Mr. Masterson makes a habit out of following any woman anywhere. They follow him." She added in her most innocent voice, "Wasn't he on one of the trains that was robbed?"

She could feel him stiffen next to her. "Which one? Seems like there's a train a day being robbed somewhere."

"Come now, you had to have heard, Mr. Parker." They turned onto the street leading to the city center. "All those robberies, and the last one with that awful murder." She pretended to shudder. "Murdered just like poor Mr. Abernathy." They stopped in front of the livery stable. "What a horrible way to die. I think I'd rather be shot."

"Well, I don't know as I would say that," he said thoughtfully, handing her down from the buggy. "Guns are noisy and smelly and too often it takes too long for the guy that gets shot to die. Now, a knife to the throat, if the guy who's holding it knows what he's doing, is quick and quiet and so long as you stay out of range of the blood spray, it's pretty efficient and, unless you're dumb enough to get caught in the act, pretty anonymous. But from the victim's point of view, and again if it's done properly—" he grinned at her and this time she could clearly see the taunt in it "—it's quick and quiet and the victim probably knew very little about it before he passed."

"You seem to know a lot about it." She stood very still, her hand trapped in his. "A better word might be efficient."

"It might at that." He made as if to kiss her again. This time she divined his intent and dodged him successfully, so he winked instead. "Like I told you, darlin'. We're all killers here."

It took a serious effort of will to turn away from him and walk toward the House, keeping her steps sure and steady.

She had a feeling he didn't buy it. Something told her he'd frightened people with effect before, and it turned out she was no exception.

She was tying her apron as she came down the stairs. The steward in charge gave her an angry look but refrained from dressing her down in front of the customers. Elizabeth was not so reticent, whispering angrily, "Where have you been? We're being run off our feet here!"

"I'm so sorry," she whispered back, and was lost in a blur of mad activity, orders taken, delivered, tables cleared, big smiles for the next customers.

It was an hour before she realized Henrietta wasn't there.

Surely she must be mistaken.

Without advertising it she checked the kitchen, made an excuse to visit the lavatory, checked outside on the platform where the girls took it in turn to catch their breath and a breath of fresh air, rare free moments during their shifts which, while not strictly authorized, were seen as acceptable by management so long as the customers didn't suffer any lack of attention.

No trace of Henrietta.

She waited for her moment, when both she and Florence were in the midst of resetting a table.

"Oh drat," Florence said, "I'm missing a napkin."

"Here, I have an extra."

"Oh, thank you, Clare." With every moment assigned a specific task, even something as minor as taking the time to fetch an additional napkin from the linen closet could put you behind.

Clare didn't tell her she'd filched it from Florence's pile in the first place. "Florence, where is Henrietta?"

Florence looked at her, startled. "Didn't you know?"

"Know what?"

"That's right, you had the afternoon off." Florence brushed back a wisp of hair. "She quit."

"She what?"

"She quit. She told Mr. Sorenson that she was quitting as of that moment, went upstairs, packed her bag, and hopped the next train north."

Sorenson? For a moment Clare's mind was blank. Oh, yes, the steward Fred Harvey had installed in Abernathy's place until he could find and train a new manager. A little thing like murder would not keep the Harvey Houses from running as on time as ATSF's trains. "But there aren't any more passenger trains north until the noon train tomorrow!"

"Ida said she talked the hoghead into letting her ride in the engine." Florence shook her head, not without relish. "Ida said Henrietta seemed like she was in an awful hurry. Something must have happened, maybe a family emergency?"

"More like a lovey-dovey one," Ida muttered.

"What do you mean?"

"She's been upset since Saturday." When Florence looked puzzled Ida huffed out an impatient breath. "When Mr. Abernathy was murdered."

"Oh." Florence's eyes widened. "Oh! You mean— But that's not allowed!"

Ida snorted. "I don't think Henrietta cared, and I know Mr. Abernathy didn't."

Watching Florence's changing expression, Clare could see that Mabel must have confided in her sister about Abernathy's visit to her house. "But Henrietta... she's been here since the day this house opened!"

From across the room Elizabeth hissed at them. "Henrietta won't be the only one on the next train north if you three don't get back to work!"

They scattered to their stations. Clare did everything as if she were an automaton, at this point seeing her customers as one giant, hungry maw into which enormous quantities of fuel must be fed for optimum output.

But she remembered the job and maintained a pleasant expression. Behind it her brain worked furiously.

Why had Henrietta felt the need to run?

If it was in fact money Parker had slipped her in the coffeehouse, why had he felt obliged to support her flight?

*We're all killers here, darlin'.*

She shuddered, and felt as if she had been recalled to life.

"You going to set those dishes down so I can wash 'em, miss?"

She woke to the fact that she was standing stock-still in the kitchen, next to the dishwashing station, the dishwasher eyeing her askance. She set down the tray, went to collect another setting, and carried it into the dining room.

It was emptying out now, and she looked up at the wall clock to see that it was close to eight o'clock, closing time.

Florence greeted her with a tired smile. "Almost done for the day, hallelujah. Mr. Sorenson telegraphed to Kansas City and told them we needed three more girls, one to replace Henrietta and two more because we need them."

"Trust a man to state the obvious," Elizabeth said, her lips pressed together in a thin line. "And wear us to the bone before getting to it."

"You're wanted at the counter," Ida said. All three of them looked at her. She smirked. "Clare." She jerked her head.

All four of them turned to look, to see Wash Gowan sitting on a stool. He looked oddly awkward, perhaps even a little tentative, as compared to when he was acting as host at his own table.

"Go on." Ida elbowed Clare. "He asked me to send you over."

"Oooooooh," Florence said, Ida joining in the chorus, both of them giggling. Elizabeth gave Clare a long, steady look. When Clare raised her eyebrows, Elizabeth shrugged and walked away with much the same determined indifference as she'd had when Clare saw her through the window of the coffeehouse. She wondered again if Elizabeth had seen her with Bat, and if she had, what that considering stare had meant. On the whole she was glad she didn't have time to ask.

She bared her teeth. "Smile check?"

Florence smoothed back an errant hair. "Fine. Perfect. Go on now." She took Clare by the shoulders, turned her around, and actually gave her a little push.

Clare managed to catch herself before stumbling and forbore from sending Florence a glare. She walked behind the counter. At this hour he was the only one left sitting at it. Come to that, he was the last customer left in the restaurant.

"Mr. Gowan." Her voice sounded flat and she knew she had to look exhausted but she was too tired to care.

"Miss Wadsworth. It's nice to see you again."

"That's right, you've been gone."

He faked a disappointed look. "You didn't miss me, then."

She gave a short laugh. "Frankly, sir, we have all been far too busy to keep track of who is here and who isn't."

"I see."

She remembered he was still a suspect and summoned a smile from somewhere. "I'm sorry, that wasn't very polite, was it? I beg your pardon." She rubbed a hand across her forehead with a weariness that was not altogether feigned. "It was known that the Harvey Girls were serving guests during your at-home. The murder of Mr. Abernathy brought in all of Montaña Roja and I would guess also people from Fort Union to Santa Fe to eat up every scrap of gossip as a side dish to their meals." She closed her eyes briefly and shook her head. "And of course we don't know anything, and no one has been caught and charged with the crime, which only adds to the gossip and speculation."

"You had the afternoon off, at least."

"Is Mr. Clemens still with you?"

"No, Clemens left on Monday."

"I'm sorry to hear it. I liked him."

"He sent you his regards."

She felt a glow. "He did?"

He laughed. "He did. You made quite the impression." He looked down at his cup. "Reyes tells me that you paid a call on Mrs. Funston."

"Yes, I did. Florence did not get the afternoon off so I drove out to check up on her. She makes amazing jumbles."

"Indeed, she does."

"Well, sir, what can I get for you?" She glanced at the wall clock. "It's almost closing time but if you're hungry I'm sure Chef would be happy to put together a quick meal."

He shook his head. "No, nothing, thank you." He hesitated. "I... wondered if you might join me for dinner one evening soon."

She wondered how genuine that tentative expression was.

"That way you could sample more of Mrs. Funston's cooking. It is superb, I assure you."

"I need no such assurance, sir, as I remember well the delicacies she prepared for your at-home." When he looked disappointed she relented and showed it. "But yours is a very kind invitation, and I am honored to accept."

His expression lightened. "I'm delighted to hear it."

She raised an admonitory finger. "It will be dependent on my work schedule. I'm told a request has been sent up the high iron for more Harvey Girls. After they arrive, we should have more time off for recreational pursuits."

He laughed. "That's the first time I've been referred to as a recreational pursuit. I'll have to make the dinner worth your while."

She didn't quite flutter her eyelashes. "I doubt that will be difficult."

He chuckled and off he went, not quite whistling but certainly with a swing in his step.

She made sure to watch him until he was on the other side of the door before she allowed the smile to drop from her face.

There was a rush of footsteps and she was surrounded by Harvey Girls. "What?" "What did he want?" "What did he say?" "What did he ask you?"

She waved them off. "It was nothing. He just wanted to make sure we were all right after Saturday."

"You were all right, maybe," Ida said, and the rest of them laughed, excited by this show of care and concern for one of their own by the town's leading citizen.

"Ladies," an awful voice said from the kitchen door, "be pleased not to idle away the rest of the evening. There are still tables to be set, those urns could use some attention, and I've set aside silverware that needs polishing."

They scattered to their duty, Clare claiming the urn-polishing because it was a one-woman job and she needed time to think.

She had to speak with Henrietta. Which meant she would have to follow her north and try to pick up her trail. Which meant she would have to leave word for Fred Harvey.

She finished the first urn and it glittered like pure silver in the light of the incandescent bulbs. She saw Florence's image reflected in its shiny surface and she turned to beckon her over.

In a moment Florence was at her side with an inquiring expression. "What?"

Clare kept her voice above a whisper, just. "Could you come to my room after work?"

"Why?"

"I drove out to see Mabel this afternoon. She sent you some jumbles."

Florence brightened. "Why didn't you say so? I'll follow you up." She winked. "I might even share."

Florence sprawled on Clare's bed, the box of jumbles open in her lap. "Oh, yes." She closed her eyes over the taste of a mouthful of cookie. "Mabel's jumbles are even better than our mother's."

"She said yours are just as good."

Florence's eyes popped open. "She did?"

"She did." Clare pulled the rocking chair around to where she could sit with her feet propped on the edge of her bed. "Ooooooh, that feels so good."

"Doesn't it, though? I feel as if I've walked all the way to Kansas and back over the last three days."

Clare wriggled her toes and wondered what kind of job she could get where she never had to wear shoes again.

"How was Mabel?" Florence said. "I haven't seen her since Saturday." She closed her eyes briefly. "I was so glad she was gone before Mr. Abernathy's body was found."

Because you were afraid she might have killed him, Clare thought, remembering Florence's white face when she recognized the victim. But Clare was certain enough in her own mind that Mabel had killed neither Abernathy nor her husband, and this conversation was not about alienating the only person she could ask for help. "She seemed fine." Clare hesitated. "She told me about Abernathy."

"She did, did she?"

Clare nodded. "He will not be much missed. By anyone." Including Fred Harvey, she thought.

"An awful man. Worse than Harry." Florence hesitated, looking at Clare. "Did you know about him and Henrietta?"

"Yes. I... saw them together."

Florence made a face. "Ugh."

"I'll say. You're sure she didn't say something today about why she was leaving or where she was going?"

"I'm sure, Clare. Why?"

Clare had rehearsed in her head all through the dinner shift how to say this, and it had never once come out right. Florence was an innocent, fresh-faced, happy-go-lucky girl fresh off the farm, thoroughly enjoying her first taste of freedom and the sweet satisfaction of earning her own money. Clare liked her. She didn't want to lie to her.

"Clare?" Florence seemed absorbed in the jumbles.

"Yes?"

"Would this have something to do with the pistol you were carrying when you found Mr. Abernathy's body?"

Clare looked up. Florence looked curious, even excited, and not at all horrified. It was enough to make up her mind. "Florence, I need to ask you for a favor, and for that I must tell you the truth."

Somewhere far, far away, in the direction of Chicago, Clare heard the B's bellow simultaneously in outrage and protest.

Florence sat up straight, dumping the box of jumbles upside down on Clare's bed. Neither of them noticed. "You're not a Harvey Girl, are you? Not a real one, I mean. You're in Montaña Roja for some other reason."

Clare blinked. "I beg your pardon?"

Florence waved an impatient hand. "You came through training, that's obvious, and you do the job, but with only half your attention. The other half is on us, on the customers, especially the customers at Mr. Gowan's table. You're not unfriendly, but you keep us all at a distance, which is not normal for a Harvey Girl. We're in this together, except for you. You disappeared from the Lightfoot for an hour with no explanation, and you stopped Abernathy from attacking Ida—oh yes, she recognized your voice and she told us. Bat Masterson calls you sweetheart and you didn't meet him for the first time yesterday if what Elizabeth saw of the two of you in the coffeehouse is even halfway true. You carry a derringer in a secret pocket in your dress and you handle it like you've used it before. And—" Florence leaned forward "—I saw you pass that note to Mr. Harvey."

Clare blinked at her. "You have been keeping a close eye on me." She thought. "All of you have." She couldn't keep the note of accusation from her voice.

Florence started putting the jumbles back in their box. "It's not that big a House, Clare, or that big a town." She put the lid on the box. "Now, are you going to tell me what's going on, and what it has to do with Henrietta?"

## 15

"I don't know why you're making such a fuss. It's barely a graze."

April 10, 1890

Thursday

The next morning Clare packed her bag, leaving her uniform hanging in the closet. There was no pang of regret at leaving it behind. Her derringer and her notebook were a reassuring weight against her leg. She pinned on her hat just as doors began to open in the hall outside. She heard Florence, Ida and Elizabeth, Mr. Sorenson and the other steward, and distantly the sound of the kitchen crew.

The minutes ticked by. The kitchen crew had been up for two hours and the smells of breakfast wafting upward made her stomach growl. There was chatter and the clatter of footsteps receding down the inside staircase.

She heard Florence's voice. "Oh, drat, I forgot— I'll be right there!"

"Hurry up!" Elizabeth. Of course.

Only a few minutes later a soft knock sounded at her door.

She cracked the door. "They're all downstairs," Florence whispered.

Clare whipped out into the hall, hearing Florence close the door behind her. She kept to the side of the hallway until she reached the door to the outside, opened it and stepped out onto the stairs.

She looked over her shoulder to see Florence in the open door. "You remember it all?" Florence nodded. "As far as anyone else is concerned, you haven't seen me or talked to me and you know nothing. You tell it only to him when he gets here."

"I understand, Clare. Go!" Florence closed the door with a click and the metal-on-metal scrape of the bolt sliding home.

Clare kept to the side of the building as she went down the stairs, just in case Florence had missed someone and they were looking out the window. She went around to the platform and hurried to the station. The telegraph office was open twenty-four hours a day and the night clerk was still on and half-asleep. He woke up when she tapped at the window. "I'd like to send a telegram, please."

He perked up when he saw a pretty girl smiling at him but he was still groggy and it took him a moment to find a blank form. Clare tried not to dance with impatience.

He handed her the form and a pencil and she filled it out quickly, addressing it to Fred Harvey in Kansas City because she didn't know where he was and they would.

*Return MR at once. See Sellers.*

She signed it "CW" and pushed it beneath the grille.

The clerk stared at it with a bemused expression. "Only six words? Uh, you still have to pay the base rate."

"Which is?"

"Forty cents."

She handed him the coins. "Could you send that at once, please? And I would like a confirmation of receipt."

There wasn't any other traffic. She waited, watching through the window as he tapped it out on the telegraph key. He brought her a slip of paper with place, time, and date and his initials scribbled at the bottom. "Thank you so much," she said with another brilliant smile. She tucked away the receipt and stepped back from the window.

"Miss?" He pressed his face up against the grille. "Do you ever go to the Lightfoot Dance Parlor?"

She turned and walked backward. "I do. Shall I see you there this evening?"

"Yes! Hey! My name is Charlie!"

"Thanks, Charlie!"

She went around into the station to find the station agent, an older man in a suit with brass buttons he kept properly shined. "Sir, may I ask you when the first train north arrives this morning?"

He sized her up without offering offense and said, "You won't be interested in the first one."

"Why not?"

"It's all livestock, no passenger cars."

"What time will it get here?"

He consulted his watch and compared it to the wall clock, a twin of the one on the tower outside but half the size. "An hour from now."

She, too, looked at the clock. It was Thursday, which meant the bank opened at eight a.m. "I'll be back."

"Miss, I can't sell you a ticket on that train. There are no seats."

"I know." She smiled at him, too. "Thank you!"

She hurried out, around the opposite side of the station so she wouldn't be seen from the Harvey House, and crossed the street.

The last train north had been at three a.m., another freighter. She would have been on it if she could have but she needed cash in hand if she was going to follow Henrietta, and unlike the telegraph office the bank wasn't open all night.

If she could manage to catch up to Henrietta and persuade her to tell what she knew, she could convince Harvey to leave the case open.

As for no seats on the next train, if Henrietta Major could talk her way onto the engine, so could Clare Wright. If she was lucky, it could even be the same engineer.

She ducked around a horse and wagon whose driver, a boy in overalls who looked ten years old and almost as awake as the telegraph operator. The ten-year-old was nodding off over the reins. In comparison, the pair of horses looked wide awake and as if they knew where they were going.

She fetched up in front of the bank and checked the hours. Yes, it opened at eight on Thursdays. Something to do with the payrolls for the mines, she had overheard someone say at some table she had waited on.

She stopped to catch her breath, check her cap, and shake out her skirt. She took a deep breath, grasped the ornate brass handle, and entered. The guard inside tipped his hat and she nodded at him and went to stand at the teller's window with the shortest line.

As early as she was, there were those who were earlier. All three windows were open and half the people in line were miners. There was one woman besides Clare, a woman a newspaper reporter would have described as "well nourished," dressed in a long and somewhat dilapidated black coat with a deep red silk flounce peeping out from beneath the hem. She turned her head when Clare came in. She had bad teeth, dyed hair, a large felt beauty mark pasted near the corner of her mouth, and shadows beneath her eyes that spoke of a long night on the job. She smiled.

Clare smiled back and the man in between them looked disapproving. Clare rolled her eyes. The other woman laughed and the man looked affronted.

The teller, a thin young man in shirtsleeves with garters and a green eyeshade, accepted the woman's deposit with neither disapproval nor affront—money was money whoever deposited it—and wrote her a receipt. "Thank you, Mrs. Cusey."

"Thank you, Ernest," she said. She turned toward the door and paused next to Clare. "I've got a place for you in my house, miss."

The man in front of her harrumphed, sounding just like Robert Pinkerton.

Clare said, "I appreciate the offer, ma'am, but I have a job."

Mrs. Cusey raised an eyebrow. "Harvey Girl?"

"Why, yes."

Mrs. Cusey sighed. "So was I once. There's a certain look." She shook her head disapprovingly. "Hard work for too little pay."

"It definitely is hard work."

"Well. If you change your mind." Mrs. Cusey walked away, her silk flounce slipping over the granite floor with a lovely swishing sound.

The man in front of her harrumphed again. He had the general shape of a pigeon and could have served as a model for any Joseph Keppler cartoon in *Puck*. "You look like a respectable young person, miss. You shouldn't be speaking to the likes of that kind of woman."

Clare opened her eyes to their widest extent. "Why, whatever kind of woman would that be?"

"Harrumph!" Full of rectitude, he bellied up to the teller's window, transacted his business, and stalked past Clare with his nose as high up in the air as his thick neck would permit.

Clare stepped up to the window. "Clare Wadsworth. I'd like to make a withdrawal, please." She produced the fake birth certificate she had had made in Chicago.

"Of course, Miss Wadsworth." He handed her a slip to fill out.

The front door opened and stayed open long enough for the cold morning air to sweep through the lobby.

She heard Dudley Platt's voice from somewhere in the back. "Close that door! Immediately!"

The teller looked over Clare's shoulder. Both hands shot into the air.

Clare blinked at him.

"Everyone down on the floor!"

She turned to see two men with pistols drawn, bandanas tied over the bottoms of their faces and large-brimmed hats pulled low over their eyes.

"On the floor and nobody gets hurt. Down! Now!" A shot was fired in the air for emphasis. It hit one of the chandeliers and brought the whole thing down in a spectacular crash. Clare flinched away from the flying glass and felt a rough hand on her shoulder shoving her to the floor. She landed face down with her cheek pressing into a shard of glass. She was dimly aware that she was bleeding but she was too terrified to investigate, which would have involved moving and she was absolutely convinced she would be dead the moment after she did.

"Well, shit," the same voice said.

"Just get the damn money." The second voice was a low growl and did nothing to alleviate her fear.

Her eyes tracked slowly around the room, as much of it as she could see from her prone position. A man who had been in the next line over was sobbing, eyes squinched closed. If he couldn't see it it wasn't happening. His wife was curled into a ball, erupting with little screams in a fractured rhythm.

"Shut up that noise!"

The woman gave another little scream. Clare had heard rabbits scream like that when caught in traps.

"Jesus."

Another man had rolled against the wall, his back to the room, frozen in place, as if he believed that not moving rendered him invisible.

A movement caught her eye and she saw one of the miners reach for his holster.

The long barrel of a Peacemaker pressed into the back of his neck. "Now, now, none of that." His hand was slapped away, the pistol pulled from his holster and dropped into a gunnysack already full.

The second man stepped up to the teller's window and held a flour bag open. "Open your till. Empty it into the bag. All of it. Now."

It took the teller a moment to realize that his arms were still in the air. When he did he complied so quickly he missed the open mouth of the bag with a bundle of cash, which fell on the floor and bounced once, landing right in front of Clare.

"For chrissake." A hand swooped down to scoop it up, and paused before her face in what felt like an eternity. She didn't move a muscle. She wasn't sure she would be capable of doing so ever again.

"Oh hell." The hand disappeared and the bundle of cash with it. "Next till. Come on, move it along. Quicker you do this the quicker we're gone."

There was the sound of drawers opening and closing, the woman's little screams, no sound at all from the man who had rolled into the wall. There was a sense of motion at the corner of Clare's eye and she looked to see the heel of a man's boot pull in behind the last desk next to the back wall. From beneath the desk she could see the shine of someone's staring eyes, and after a befuddled moment realized it was Dudley Platt, the bank manager, with his face pressed against the floor, his body crammed into the kneehole of the desk, his hands over his ears. He saw her looking at him and squeezed his eyes closed.

"That all of it?"

"That's it."

"Okay, let's go." The robber raised his voice. "Boys, we'll leave your guns outside. Don't rush to get them, okay? Nobody's got hurt yet and we'd like to keep it that way."

The one who had spoken looked down at her and winked and headed for the door.

He winked at her.

He *winked*.

Rage, welcome, warming, flooded through her body and in a single motion she sat up, drew her derringer and fired.

The robber stumbled and staggered a few steps. "Ouch! What the hell! Goddamn it! Goddamn son of a bitch!" A hand came up and clutched his opposite arm. "Fuck! Shit! That hurt!"

He turned and reached down his bloodied hand and hauled her to her feet and dragged her after him out of the bank. She did not go quietly and when he got to the horses, two of which were being held by a third man Clare had never seen before, she was tossed over a saddle, the horn gouging her painfully in the stomach. All the breath left her body in a whoosh. The robber swung up behind her and the horses were kicked from a standing start into a full gallop.

"What the hell do you think you're doing?" the other robber yelled over the thunder of hooves.

"She shot me!"

"So what! Let her go!"

"She made the mess, she can clean it up!"

"You are a goddamn fool!"

"Don't I know it!"

They galloped through town, scattering people in front of them until they reached the city limits, when the robbers bent forward and urged their mounts faster. Clare's face hung upside down and banged against the rider's leg and her head swam as the blood pooled in her brain. The saddle horn bruised her stomach every time the horse's hooves struck the ground. She gathered up all of her energy and managed to speak. "Damn you! Let! Me! GO!"

All she received in reply was a breathless laugh that sounded almost giddy and a smack on her behind. She gritted her teeth and refused to protest further, because she knew it would have come out in an indignant squeal.

They rode on without stopping and without slackening their speed. By a miracle none of the three horses stumbled into a prairie dog hole. After an eternity, or what Clare later reckoned was ten minutes, they slowed and then stopped. Clare was unceremoniously dumped to the ground, where she landed hard on her back and almost beneath the horses' hooves. She rolled away and scrambled to her feet, finding the front of her jacket and skirt soaked through by the horse's sweat.

She looked up, dazed and a little dizzy. Her hat was dangling by a hairpin from the back of her head and she pulled it free with shaking hands. "You—you—"

Her kidnapper pulled off his bandana. "Here," Bob Parker said, shoving it at her. "Tie me up."

She stared at the bandana. "Are you joking?"

He shoved the bandana into her hands. "Get it done."

"You expect me to—"

Bob Parker held up his arm, nearly rubbing her face in his wound and she jerked back. "Tie it up, dammit! You shot me, you fix it!"

The other robber's voice was sure and steady as he pulled his saddle from his mount's heaving flanks. "Robert LeRoy Parker, I know your mama taught you to treat a woman better than that."

"She shot me!"

"You shouldn't have winked at me," she said. "I didn't know for sure it was you until you did."

He stared at her. "You shot me because I winked at you?"

She rolled up his sleeve, folded the bandana and wrapped it around his wound. "I don't know why you're making such a fuss. It's barely a graze."

"You can say that, you're not the one who got shot!"

She looked past him at the second robber, who had now also removed his bandana. Fred Parker had finished saddling his fresh horse and was engaged in knotting two flour bags full of cash together. He slung them over the saddle behind the horn.

There was another fresh horse waiting for Bob, leading rein held by Georgie the murderer, who looked nervous and wouldn't meet her eye.

The remains of a dry camp with a fire ring made of rocks could be seen through the trees. There were a couple of empty canvas bags on the ground that Clare remembered seeing tied to Georgie's saddle, then filled with water.

The ex-sheriff of Montaña Roja tossed a bundle of cash to Georgie and another to the man who had been waiting outside the bank. "Georgie, Sawtooth, thanks, boys. You better hump. They'll be right behind us."

The two of them did not need telling twice. They slapped the reins against their horses' flanks and literally headed for the hills, the foothills of the Sangre de Cristo

Mountains. The range swallowed both of them whole almost instantaneously, leaving nothing of their passage behind but hoofprints and a trace of dust hanging in the air.

She knotted the bandana and stepped back, trying and failing to rub the blood from her hands. "Did you kill Abernathy?"

He pulled down his sleeve and swung into the saddle. He grinned at her. "Just tying up loose ends, darlin'. What any good thief does when his plan goes south."

"Did you rob the trains?" He robbed banks, she thought. A train was just another target, albeit a moving one.

He looked blank for just long enough for her to notice it. He recovered almost immediately and laughed. "Well, hell, darlin'. You're just all full of ideas now, aren't you?" He cocked his head. "Although now that I think of it, the trains move plenty of cash, now, don't they? What do you think, Uncle Fred? Should we move up to robbing trains?"

Fred Parker's horse danced a little beneath an incautiously driven heel. "You start robbing trains, Bob, you're on your own. I warned you this was a one-time deal. Wouldn't a done it if not for Mary and the kids."

She stared at him askance. He was as sober today as the night he had danced with her at the Lightfoot Dance Parlor.

"Aw c'mon, Uncle Fred, I'm just jollying the girl along. She thinks she knows most of it already anyway. This ain't some ordinary Harvey Girl, this one." He cocked an eyebrow. "Damn if I know what she is, though."

She stared at him, and thought back to the first time she'd seen both of them, on the platform outside the Harvey House. Bob catching Fred before he fell. Bob sliding in between them at the end of that waltz, when the expression on Fred's face had, just for a moment, made her feel almost... disposable, was the only word that came to her mind.

He was looking at her that way now, she realized. He had every motive to do so. She knew who they were and she could absolutely identify them. One shot to her head, a quick grave off the trail, and leave her for the wild creatures to erase any evidence of her existence.

The only way she knew how to move forward was to do so. She mustered her outrage and hoped no trace of fear showed in her expression. "And Funston?"

He shrugged. "You already think the worst of me, darlin'. Not gonna waste my breath saying it ain't so. Ready, Uncle Fred?"

"Ready."

Bob jerked his chin at the horses. "You can walk them back, darlin.' Give 'em a good cooling off."

He winked at her. If she hadn't already spent the derringer's single charge shooting him the first time she would have shot him again.

Fred actually touched the brim of his hat. "Ma'am."

They kicked their horses into motion, galloped over the other side of the knoll and headed for a distant stand of cottonwoods. There would be water there, Clare thought longingly, and more fresh horses. She watched until the roll of the high desert hid them from sight.

The first thing she did was reload her derringer. He hadn't even searched her for it.

She sighed and rubbed her stomach. It hurt. There would be bruises. Her hair was straggling and thick with dust and she was sweating through her jacket as the sun rose inexorably toward high noon.

She couldn't find it in her heart to subject either of the exhausted horses to the burden of her weight. It annoyed her to fall in with Bob's suggestion but she took the reins of each and began walking them to town. It had shrunk on the horizon to a collection of unnatural shapes that shimmered in the rising heat.

The distance was a lot longer on foot than it was on horseback, and a lot drier, too. She plodded on, a little bent over because her stomach hurt from the saddle horn. A snake rattled nearby and one of the horses whinnied and the other one snorted and danced. Clare quieted them and then picked up a rock and heaved it at the diamondback, not with any real intention of hitting it but as a means of discouragement. It slithered off looking disgruntled.

"No more than me," she said out loud. Her mouth was so dry she could barely articulate the words. Marcy's *Prairie Traveler* had six pages on snakes, filled with what to do if you were bitten by one. She recalled one line in particular: *Of all the remedies known to me, I should decidedly prefer ardent spirits.*

So would Clare in the present moment. Spirits were liquid.

They trudged on, the horses' heads hanging in exhaustion and the sweat drying on their withers beneath the rising temperature. As when she was hanging upside down over Parker's saddle horn, minutes seemed to elongate on their own into hours. The morning breeze had died. She stopped to rest frequently, and wished she had water to give the horses and herself, but the river was a long way off and she would not deviate from the straightest way back to town for any inducement. If she had to she would climb up on one of the poor creatures and trust it to find its way home, but she wasn't yet that far gone.

She had no idea how much time had passed before she saw a cloud of dust approaching from the south. It felt like a much longer time had passed after that hopeful sign before she heard the hoofbeats.

She looked up to see a large group of men on horseback riding hell for leather straight at her. She led the horses to the side of the trail and waited.

They slowed down when they saw her. Bat Masterson was in the lead and he swung his right leg over the saddle and rode the horse to a stop with his left foot still in the stirrup. He dropped down and came forward. "Are you all right, sweetheart?"

It annoyed her that he looked as elegant as he ever did, not a hair out of place, not a speck of dust on his suit, his derby not a degree off its habitual jaunty angle. "Yes. I'm fine. They had horses waiting on the track up ahead. The young man who shot his partner in front of the saloon last month? He was waiting with them."

Dudley Platt, last seen crouching beneath his desk, said, "Which way were they headed, ma'am?"

"North the last time I saw them. They had remounts waiting." She gestured at the two horses she led. "These were the ones they left town on."

"Why did they take you?"

She looked at Bat and made a face. "I shot one of them."

There was a stir at this. "You what?"

She looked at the banker. "You were there, Mr. Platt. Didn't you see?"

"I heard a shot. I didn't realize it was you shooting."

She remembered he had his eyes closed and his hands over his ears. Probably best not to mention that. "I think he was just mad at me for shooting him. He made me dress his wound." She looked at her hands, still stained with Bob Parker's blood. "Upper right arm, only a graze. I was a little upset. I think it affected my aim."

"Who was it? Did you know them?"

"Oh yes, I knew them. I danced with both of them at the Lightfoot Dance Parlor two weeks ago. We all did. So did your wives and daughters. One was Bob Parker, Mr. George Washington Gowan's foreman. The other was Sheriff—" she emphasized the title and repeated it just to be clear "—Sheriff Fred Parker. Your sheriff. The sheriff of Montaña Roja."

There was another stir at this. "You coming?" Platt said to Masterson.

"You go on after them. I'll escort the lady back to town, see she comes to no more harm."

Platt looked at him for a moment. The horses stamped and their harness creaked and clinked. Their riders looked impatient. Platt said, "I hear tell you've been a sheriff a time or two, Masterson."

"I have."

"And that you know one end of a gun from the other."

"I do."

Platt looked north for a long moment, and then back at Bat. "It appears Montaña Roja needs someone to step up and take the badge. Would you be interested? On a temporary basis?"

Bat thought about it and in the end shrugged. "Why not?"

Platt nodded. "I'll see you at the sheriff's office when we get back to town. I don't expect this to take long."

Bat glanced at Clare. Neither of them shared the banker's confidence.

The posse moved out, sans some half of their number who, now that the fair maiden had rescued herself, headed back toward town. One dropped toward the back of this group and then out of it completely, unnoticed by the rest. He turned and came back.

"Hello, Tom," she said.

He unhooked his canteen from the saddle and handed it down. "You sure you're all right?"

"I'm fine." The two men exchanged a glance. "I'm fine, truly, I'm fine. He didn't hurt me. I hurt him and I'm glad of it." She unscrewed the cap of the canteen and drank long and deep. The water was warm and tasted of minerals but it was wet and so very welcome to the flesh of her mouth and throat.

"I was so scared. And then I was so mad." She took another long drink. "I promise you, I wasn't aiming at his arm." She looked around. Tom doffed his hat and handed it to her. She turned it upside down and poured water from the canteen into it, offering it to the horses in turn until the canteen was empty. She capped it and handed both back to Tom and started down the trail again. At this point all she wanted was a bath and a bed. Neither man offered her his mount, which showed how well both of them knew her.

Tom nudged his horse into a slow walk. "Anger always screws up your aim."

"Did either one of them say anything about the train robberies?" Bat said, walking next to her, his horse's reins in his hand.

"I asked Bob if he killed Abernathy, and Funston. He said he was tidying up loose ends, what you do when a plan goes sour. But—"

"But what?"

She didn't think Bob Parker had killed either Funston or Abernathy. She did think he cared about his uncle, though. Enough to take the blame for murders he hadn't committed? "I asked him if he'd robbed the trains and he just grinned that dimple grin of his and shrugged his shoulders. Said I thought the worst of him already and he wasn't going to waste time trying to convince me otherwise."

She saw them exchange another glance. "What?"

"This wasn't his first bank robbery, sweetheart," Bat said. "Well, it wasn't Bob's. I don't know about the sheriff."

She halted. "I beg your pardon?"

They stopped and he faced her with a rueful expression. "He robbed the San Miguel Valley Bank in Telluride last June. Got away clean with twenty thousand." He jerked his thumb over his shoulder. "Did it just like this time, had remounts waiting in stages. I'll allow it was pretty slick all around. Posse never did catch up with him."

"How do you know this?"

"When I was sheriffing up in Trinidad, the sheriff of Ouray came through on some business or other. Told me the tale. Said the sheriff of Telluride was on vacation at the time of the robbery. Everyone figured it was a vacation paid for by the bank robbers."

She sighed. "This time he saved money by putting a relative on staff."

"Looks like."

"Why didn't you tell me this before?"

He looked at her, his mouth a straight line. "He knows plenty about me, too, sweetheart."

"What? How? What are you talking about?"

He squinted at the sun. She followed his gaze. It wasn't even noon yet. "Gonna get hot soon. We best get on into town."

"I'll ride on ahead." Tom looked down at her. "Are we done here?"

"I don't know."

"I'll send a telegram to Chicago. See if they want me to stick around. You're safe, so my job's done."

She halted, staring up at him. "What did you say?"

He urged his horse into a trot.

She turned to Bat. "What did he say?"

He shook his head and took the horses' reins from her hand. "I told you, sweetheart. The B's do set some store by you."

## 16

"Yours were not the only goods being stolen, Mr. Harvey."

*Montaña Roja, New Mexico Territory*

APRIL 14, 1890

MONDAY

Fred Harvey heard her out in silence. At the end he poured her a glass of water. "You do ride a little close to the wind, Miss Wright."

He handed her the glass and she sipped gratefully. Her throat still felt parched. If she had learned nothing else from her experiences in the New Mexico Territory, it was never to allow herself to be abducted without a supply of water. "No closer than I need to to get the job done, Mr. Harvey. I didn't kidnap myself, you know."

He went to stand in front of the window that looked out on the busy Kansas City street. "I'm glad you suffered no serious injury."

"A few bruises, no more." She sipped from her glass. "Is there any news of Henrietta Major?"

He shook his head. "The hoghead said she got off in Kansas City. She could have gone anywhere from there. I've sent telegrams up and down the high iron. No one with her name or matching her description has been seen in any of the Harvey Houses. Do you really think she might have had something to do with any of this?"

He was very nearly begging her to say no. "She was on intimate terms with Abernathy, and I saw Parker give her money."

"Why would he do that?"

"I can only imagine that she knows something that he didn't want known by anyone else. Certainly she knows more than we do at present. When we find her, we can ask her."

His shoulders slumped. "I'll tell our people to keep looking for her."

The American West was very nearly designed for disappearing into. Clare held out little hope of ever seeing the other Harvey Girl again. She took another sip of water and schooled her expression not to look accusing, although it took some effort. "Mr. Harvey, why didn't you tell me about Mabel Funston?"

He paused fractionally in replacing the pitcher, and then set it down so gently she didn't hear the glass touch the silver tray. He stood with his back to her for a few moments. She waited. If she were ever going to work with him again, she needed an answer now, and preferably a convincing one.

He turned to face her squarely and she was surprised to see that his face was flushed. "I'm sorry, Miss Wright." He grimaced. "It seems I'm always apologizing to you for some transgression." He took a deep breath. "It seemed obvious that Ma— that Mrs. Funston clearly knew nothing of what we are now assuming was her husband's collusion in the robberies." He raised his shoulders in a slight shrug. "And it seemed cruel, after her husband's death, to further harass her with questions. Three children, the loss of her family's provider..." He shook his head. "She wanted to stay near her sister, and Mr. Gowan need a cook, so I asked him as a favor to me to give her a trial. And..." He didn't quite squirm. "Well, Gowan is a single man, and she's an attractive woman, so I thought..." His voice trailed off.

Clare hid a smile. "That you would play matchmaker?"

He walked over to the window and looked out at Washington Avenue. They were in the manager's office, with the ledgers stacked neatly to one side of the desk. "Perhaps."

"I see." Clare decided a change of topic might be best, before Mr. Harvey expired of sheer embarrassment. She also wondered just how attractive he himself found Mabel Funston, and if two miles out of town seemed a safe distance to keep temptation at bay. "I wonder, Mr. Harvey, do you know who hired Fred Parker for the position of sheriff?"

He looked relieved. "I asked Mr. Gowan that exact question. On behalf of Montaña Roja's city fathers, it was Mr. Gowan who put out the word that they were looking for someone to fill that position. His new foreman—" his smile was caustic "—recommended his uncle. Mr. Platt in particular was impressed by Parker's background as a police officer in Washington, D.C."

She closed her eyes and shook her head.

"Yes," he said, "I quite agree. Tell me, Miss Wright, do you believe the Parkers acted alone?"

"They could have. Bob Parker was Mr. Gowan's foreman. In that position, he had access to any and all of Mr. Gowan's assets. He stole a dozen of his horses for remounts to escape on after he and his uncle robbed the bank."

His stare was penetrating. "But you don't think so."

She had her head down, swirling the water in the glass. "A… source told me that this was not Bob Parker's first bank robbery. The man knows how. Perhaps his previous successes made him ambitious for more. It's a big step from robbing a bank to making entire railroad cars loaded with freight disappear, but…" She took a sip of water, aware he was watching her with an assessing gaze.

"You are ominously silent, Miss Wright. You said once something about looking beyond the thefts. Is this all you meant, or is there more?"

"Well." She took a deep breath. "It is, unfortunately, a maxim in my business that wrongdoing in one instance leads almost invariably to wrongdoing in another."

"Meaning?"

"Meaning, I have had time now to thoroughly examine the Montaña Roja Harvey House ledgers. It will require a more thorough accounting than I can do, but I can tell you with every assurance that yours were not the only goods being stolen in those train robberies, Mr. Harvey."

She'd had her bath and a night's uninterrupted sleep and another full day spent going over the ledgers before Fred Harvey tornadoed his way back to Montaña Roja. Harvey had received Clare's telegram and had immediately sent another to Sorenson saying Miss Clare Wadsworth had his full confidence and for Mr. Sorenson to aid her in any way she could, no questions asked. This time she went page by page, for the two full years the Montaña Roja Harvey House had been open and for the previous six months covering its construction, as well as the construction of the ATSF stop.

While it was a little difficult to disentangle which charges for what materials went to which side of the operation, it wasn't impossible. A real auditor was needed for a thorough examination but Clare soon saw there was nothing original about Abernathy's predations. She'd found false vendors and invoices paid whose amounts were higher than what few matching bills she could find (she was certain Abernathy had destroyed many of them) in the months during construction. After the House opened, she found payroll entries showing staff front and back working sixteen, eighteen, even twenty hours a day. She had asked Elizabeth Higgins if during her work at any Harvey House she had worked any shifts that long and the answer had been an adamant "No."

"What!" Fred Harvey said now, halfway between outraged and despairing.

"I'm afraid not."

"What else was stolen? From whom?"

"I don't know. According to the bills of lading, the contents were under seal, and I'm guessing the House only has copies of those bills so they know which freight in which cars is theirs to unload. And which isn't."

"Seal? What do you mean seal? There isn't—" His voice changed. "Whose seal?"

She was very sorry to be the deliverer of this very bad news but there was no help for it. "Mr. Harvey, I'm afraid it was the seal of the United States government."

A long pause. "Which branch?"

"The Department of War. In this case the United States Army."

"Where were they going?"

"Every one of the missing cars had been en route to Fort Union."

Another long silence. When he spoke again Harvey's voice was almost pleading. "But that's nonsense, Miss Wright. There hasn't been a word about any missing supplies or—" his voice faltered a little "—or matériel headed for the Army at Fort Union. Believe me, there would have been, and believe me when I tell you I would have heard of it."

She absorbed this in silence for a moment. "Are you quite sure of that, Mr. Harvey?"

"Quite sure," he said, although he sounded less certain of it than either of them would have preferred.

"I see." She sighed. "Then we can only assume that either the government is aware of the missing cars and their contents and wish to keep this news silent for reasons of their own, or…"

"Or?"

"Or," she said steadily, "someone at Fort Union is well aware of the thefts and is colluding in them and covering them up. And I'm afraid that I find that fact almost as interesting as the fact that there are missing supplies." She turned to look at him and added softly, "And so should you be."

He scowled. "Was the theft of the cars holding our goods only a cover for the theft of the cars carrying the supplies bound for Fort Union?"

She took her time answering and when she did she spoke with care. "I believe it was Napoleon who said that an army travels on its stomach."

He paced to the fireplace, stood, irresolute for a moment, and came back to stand before her. "What would you do first, to find these missing supplies?"

"I would find a way to spend time in Fort Union. Someone there knows something, maybe not where the cars are, or where the supplies went. But something."

A long silence as each of them wrestled with their own thoughts.

Clare was not yet ready to disclose all of her suspicions, but she had seen enough of Fred Harvey to imagine that their thoughts were running on similar lines. If Bob and Fred Parker had not been involved in the train robberies, the person who had been could use the Parkers' robbing of the Montaña Roja Trust and Savings Bank as a brush to tar them with the train robberies as well. It was certainly a conclusion Clare had jumped to. And with the guilty having escaped capture, there was no need to produce evidence of their complicity. Just saying it, as many times as possible to as many people as possible, would be enough to deflect attention from the real thieves.

And the real thieves' motive.

She heard Reyes' voice in her head.

*He came here to meet with Mr. Gowan.*

Clare had assumed that Harry Funston had come to the ranch to meet with Bob Parker, who had access to all the resources necessary to rob the trains. But what if Reyes was speaking the exact truth, and Funston had come to meet with Wash Gowan?

"What? What are you thinking of now, Miss Wright?"

She looked up to see Harvey staring at her, almost sternly. Authority over a case remained with the agent in charge, and here in this moment that agent in charge was Clare. She owed him the truth. At the same time, she didn't want to alienate the man whose whole company would be affected by what she did next, so she picked over her next words very carefully. "Mr. Harvey, I think something much uglier and more frightening is going on here."

Her eyes held a clear warning and he looked away, his jaw clenched. After a moment he said, "Well? What do you think is going on here, then?"

"I think," she said, softly but inexorably, "that those stolen supplies went to support activities across the border."

"What activities?"

She shrugged. "Read the front page of any newspaper. There's a story every other day about Rockefeller drilling for oil south of the border, or Morgan digging for copper. All President Díaz asks in return is a slice of the profits. There have to be plenty of Mexican citizens who don't like it that the Guggenheims aren't paying Mexican taxes on the Mexican silver they're taking out of Mexico. Hard not to picture an interested party taking advantage of that unrest to pursue goals of their own."

Such as, say, someone who had collected a roomful of royal regalia, who might also harbor the ambition to one day wear it.

Harvey looked a little taken aback. "You seem to know a lot about Mexican affairs."

"Part of the job. I had a month during training in Kansas City to read up on the New Mexico Territory. ATSF tracks run straight to El Paso, where they connect with the Mexican Central Railway. With Funston and Abernathy's knowledge and experience, and a little money to, ah, influence Mexican customs, it wouldn't have been difficult to connect a line of cars to an engine with no questions asked and no official notice taken, and make them disappear."

"Why didn't they put you in management?" She looked at him, unable to hide her surprise, and he gave her an apologetic look. "I'm sorry, but you have his eyes. I noticed it in Chicago the day we met. And your features—" He made a vague gesture towards her face. "Impossible to miss the resemblance." Her expression made him look away. "I apologize if I am intruding on your privacy."

"I didn't want to be in management," she said, when she was certain her voice would remain even.

His smile was faint. "Don't like working under a roof. I remember." He hesitated. "So, Robert and William are your..."

"Half-brothers."

He nodded, eyes on her face. He was curious, naturally so, but she didn't get the feeling he was prying, just interested. She set the glass to one side and folded her hands. "My mother was the first woman detective Allan Pinkerton hired." Her chin came up. "She was on President Lincoln's security detail."

"Before—"

Her lips came together in a thin line. "Oh yes, well before." She felt the weight of the derringer in the pocket of her skirt. The same make and model that had killed President Lincoln.

"So you followed in your mother's footsteps."

"Yes. She died when I was born. Allan—" not "my father," never "my father" "—provided for my education and left me some money in his will. But I wanted to work, and I didn't want to spend my time on paperwork and filing. I wanted to work cases."

"Your mother's work."

"Yes."

"In homage to her."

"Perhaps at first." She shook her head. "Not now."

"You grew to like it for your own sake."

"I was good at it. I am good at it."

"Marriage?"

"I'm not opposed to it in principle, Mr. Harvey. Maybe. Someday."

"Children?"

"If I find the right man to be their father, yes. Unless or until I do…"

He frowned at his boots. There was an entire world in what she had left unsaid, but there was enough there that he wouldn't feel he was taking advantage of her. "I appreciate everything you've done, Miss Wright." A ghost of a smile. "You have given perfect satisfaction. Even if I don't quite know how."

She raised her shoulders in a slight shrug. "We never sleep."

His laugh was brief. "So I have seen. Well." He stood up, walked to the window and stood looking out, his hands clasped behind his back. "Since it seems the Harvey Girls hear everything first, I assume you already know of my plans to build a new eating house at Fort Union. Lunches only, at least at first, and a newsstand."

"My information has it that it is already under construction."

This time his laugh had more actual humor in it. "Indeed it is." He turned. "We don't know who is responsible for the thefts of the cars carrying supplies for Fort Union."

We might have a pretty good idea, she thought, but responded only with a slight lift of her brows.

He raised a hand to fiddle with the cord of the window blind. "Would Pinkerton extend your contract, do you think?"

"But we have completed this one," she said in a neutral tone. "And," she added, forestalling him when he would have spoken again, "if you did wish to hire me on a new case, Robert and William would insist on knowing the particulars."

"That... would not be acceptable to me."

The Pinkertons' connections to the federal government could be taken for granted. As soon as one of the B's knew something, a day later people in the White House and in Congress did, too. Still, she said, "You could make the thefts known to those with oversight responsibility in Washington."

"I could," he said, considering. "But then I would have to know who wasn't in on the theft to begin with."

"You would. Because someone certainly was somewhere along the line." There was something she had overheard. Where was it? Yes, of course, at Gowan's at-home. "I just remembered," she said slowly. "At Mr. Gowan's at-home, Señor Rubio y Castelló approached Colonel Benteen. He told him..." What had been the grandee's exact words? "He said something about the shipments being too small and too few."

"And what was the colonel's reply?"

"He refused to speak to him there and then and took his wife by the arm and led her off." She looked up to meet his eyes. "It could mean nothing."

He looked again through the window, hands clasped behind his back, appearing lost in thought.

She had a few of those herself, mostly about Mr. Harvey's great and good friend and business associate, George Washington Gowan. The memory of that gaudy trophy room returned, and what such a collection said about a man's character and aspirations. She heard Mr. Clemens' voice whisper in her ear.

*How narrowing a thing it is for a man to have wealth who makes a god of it instead of a servant.*

He had warned her in terms as clear as he could make them, although she was certain that in his context he was warning her away from romantic involvement with such a man. Avuncular advice for a young woman who had no family to watch over her. It was a kind thought, and all the more reason to remember him kindly.

She gave the back of Fred Harvey's head an appraising look, and wondered how he might take it if Gowan was found to be complicit in some way with the theft of war matériel stolen from the United States government to fuel a revolution in one of its nearest neighbors?

Harvey turned. "I was born in England, Miss Wright, but I am an American by choice. The idea of someone using the Fred Harvey name to steal food and ammunition meant for American troops sickens me. I want it stopped."

She looked down at her hands and cleared her throat. "Perhaps…"

"Yes?"

"Is it possible that you have been put on alert by recent events, and would like to ensure that they don't repeat themselves any time soon? In which case, your request for the continued presence of a Pinkerton agent would be more than justified." She met his eyes. "I assume you could make that case?"

He gave a slow nod. "I could indeed."

And the B's weren't likely to say no to any request of Fred Harvey's.

# Envoi...

JULY 17, 1890

THURSDAY

The envelope was directed to "Clare Wadsworth" care of the Fred Harvey Company in Kansas City and found its way to her without difficulty. There was no return address. Inside was the newspaper clipping of an obituary.

> **John Frederick Parker, 60, carpenter, of Washington D.C.**
>
> Born May 30, 1830, Virginia. Died of pneumonia June 28, 1890. Survived by wife Mary America Maus and three children of Washington D.C., and nephew Robert LeRoy Parker of Wyoming.

An accompanying note in the copperplate hand taught in every one-room schoolhouse in the country read

*You surely took Uncle Fred's fancy.*
*He didn't hardly even want to go home,*
*but he had to, to give his share to his family.*
*His wife ain't much but there were the kids.*
*Must have caught the old man's friend on the way back.*
*Damn trains, one person's got it, everybody's got it.*

*You only winged me, darling.*
*You could use some practice on a range.*
*I just bet old Wash would let you use his.*

*B.*

# Acknowledgements

My heartfelt thanks to Liz and Greg at Head of Zeus for catching all the typos, misspellings, and outright errors of fact I allowed to creep into my manuscript. Give them a raise, Nic!

Years ago my friends Barbara Peters and Rob Rosenwald took me to La Posada, one of the few remaining Fred Harvey hotels, this one in Winslow, Arizona (yes, of "standing on the corner" fame). In their gift shop I found a copy of Stephen Fried's *Appetite for America: Fred Harvey and the Business of Civilizing the Wild West—One Meal at a Time*. Chapter 12 is titled "Harvey Girls."

What? Who?

Until that moment I'd never heard of the Harvey Girls, the first uniformed service for women in history. It was a revelation. Fried's book brings that time and those people to full Technicolor life and is the urtext for the Clare Wright series.

But any era as romanticized as the heyday of the American West is bound to be written of many times by many authors; indeed, it often feels as if everyone who ever lived or traveled or even spent five minutes there wrote a book about it. Here follow some that have kept this novel honest.

On Fred Harvey and the Harvey Girls, the above-referenced work by Stephen Fried, *The Harvey Girls: Women Who Opened the West* by Lesley Poling-Kempes, and *Harvey Houses of New Mexico: Historic Houses of Hospitality from Raton to Deming* by Rosa Walston Latimer. There are many more, and the History Press' backlist is a first stop for anyone interested in the period. On Western women, *New Women in the Old West: From Settlers to Suffragists, an Untold American Story* by Winifred Gallagher, who has made a praiseworthy effort to include everyone. On the Pinkertons, *Inventing the Pinkertons; or, Spies, Sleuths, Mercenaries, and Thugs* by S. Paul O'Hara, *The Pinks: The First Women Detectives, Operatives, and Spies with the Pinkerton National Detective Agency* by Chris Enss, and *Pinkerton's First Lady: Kate Warne – United States First Female Detective* by John Derrig and Jennifer FitzGerald. On the railroads, John Sedgwick's *From the River to the Sea: The Untold Story of the Railroad War that Made the West*. On the Gilded Age, *The Reckless Decade: America in the 1890s* by H.W. Brands and *The Tycoons: How Andrew Carnegie, John D. Rockefeller, Jay Gould, and J.P. Morgan Invented the American Supereconomy* by Charles R. Morris. On cowboys and range wars, the acerbically written and meticulously annotated *High Noon in Lincoln: Violence on the Western Frontier* by Robert M. Utley. On Pueblo life, Alice Marriott and Margaret Lefranc's *María, the Potter of San Ildefonso*. On Porfirio Díaz and the Mexican Revolution, *Bad Mexicans: Race, Empire, and Revolution in the Borderlands* by Kelly Lytle Hernández. On the U.S. Army in the American West, Hampton Sides' *Blood and*

*Thunder* and Nathaniel Philbrick's *The Last Stand: Custer, Sitting Bull, and the Battle of the Little Big Horn.*

Obviously I've conflated disparate true events and characters in this narrative. No apologies because it was a time and place that attracted the larger than life like a magnet. Following Wyatt Earp and Bat Masterson around Dodge City is enough to make anyone duck and cover. According to Stephen Fried, Bat Masterson did in fact work for Fred Harvey for a time as security for a Harvey restaurant that kept getting robbed. He was also at one point sheriff of Trinidad, Colorado, where Damon Runyon managed a baseball team, whence cometh the *Guys and Dolls* character Skye Masterson, which I first learned of in Tom Clark's excellent biography, *The World of Damon Runyon*.

Puerperal fever was called childbed fever back in the day and infected almost a quarter of all women giving birth, although epidemics could take out a hundred percent of the patients in what were called "lying-in" hospitals. By far and away the majority of cases were due to doctors and nurses not washing their hands. Worse, in the 1800s as many as forty percent of children died at birth and if they survived to the age of ten had only a sixty percent chance of surviving into adulthood. Clare might be angry over what she perceives as her father's neglect but she was one of the lucky ones.

The story about the haunting of the Mississippi bank vice-president was inspired by a story in Enss' *The Pinks*, a real case in which the detective was the real Kate Warne, a Pinkerton agent who served on President Lincoln's security detail before there was a Secret Service. The Pinkertons weren't on duty that night in Ford's Theater; John Frederick Parker of the Washington, D.C. police force was supposed to have been.

The story about the train robberies was inspired by Brands' *The Reckless Decade*, where he asserts that most robber barons shrugged off train robberies as the price of doing business. According to Fried this was Fred Harvey's attitude, too, so I had to kill someone in order for Fred to care enough to hire Clare.

The Scottish play riot really did happen, albeit in 1849 in New York City, where people actually did die. The urge to name-check the event even in passing was irresistible. My source was Nigel Cliff's lively and frighteningly erudite *The Shakespeare Riots: Revenge, Drama, and Death in Nineteenth-Century America*.

While I have found no specific mention of Butch Cassidy robbing any Arizona banks, he certainly knew how. I modeled this robbery on his June 1889 San Miguel Valley Bank robbery in Telluride, Colorado. He was born a Mormon in Utah and his birth name was Robert LeRoy Parker. When I stumbled across the story of John Frederick Parker I succumbed to the temptation to write them both into my narrative as kin. The "old man's friend" that Butch refers to in his note was a contemporary nickname for pneumonia, as it killed a lot of them back in the day.

Mark Twain was burying his mother in Missouri around the time of this book and who's to say he didn't take a brief vacation in the Southwest afterward? All he had to do was step on a train. Much of his dialogue is taken from his own words.

I first heard of Mrs. Cusey, aka Madam Millie, from her obituary in 1993, because at one point she ran a brothel in Ketchikan, Alaska, and Alaska newspapers decided that attention must be paid. At least one Harvey Girl became a rustler, too, but that's for the next book.

Many of the above-mentioned books were found in gift shops in National Park visitor centers, which are a superb resource for reference works on the American West. The ranger at Devil's Tower raised her eyebrows at my stack whose height rivaled the mountain outside and said, "I'll give you a bag. You deserve it." That stack included *Bleed, Blister, and Purge: A History of Medicine on the American Frontier* by Volney Steele, M.D., and *Prairie Traveler* by Randolph B. Marcy, the Rick Steves of his day for the American West.

Wikipedia was an enormous help, as for example when I needed a model for Wash Gowan's mansion and there found a page of images of Gilded Age mansions by state, which then led me to the Beaux-Arts architecture page, which style seemed to suit Wash Gowan's ambitions. John Sedgwick's description of Glen Eyrie, General William Jackson Palmer's aspirational mansion in Colorado Springs, was also informative. From what I can tell most of the robber barons' homes were just about that restrained, and the apparently ineradicable habit of rich Americans using their checkbooks to loot European art and antiquities to furnish their mansions back home is as old as the nation.

Reddit and Quora were also useful, although FYI, when you begin a search for how long it takes someone to die of a cut throat, the first hits are always mental health hotlines. Need to know what time the sun rose on April 6, 1890? The U.S.

Naval Observatory has your back. Need to know what days in 1890 had a full moon? Click on over to moongiant.com. I heart the Internet.

Since that first trip to La Posada I have returned many times. I have stayed at El Tovar and Bright Angel on the south rim of the Grand Canyon, toured La Fonda in Santa Fe, and visited La Castañeda in Las Vegas, New Mexico. In 2024 I made a road trip through northern New Mexico, where in Belen the local library has managed to get hold of one of the Harvey restaurants and, miraculously, keep it, and it's still serving food! It was the perfect model for my fictional Montaña Roja Harvey House.

Too many of the Harvey Houses have been torn down (Fried's book has an appendix listing those Harvey Houses still standing and those still in operation), but there are small and not so small collections of Harvey House and Harvey Girls memorabilia in museums, parks national, state and city, and hotels all over the Southwest. There are many photographs to be found in all those places and online. You can see in two dimensions what your imagination will fill in for the third.

For nearly ninety years, where there were ATSF train tracks there was Fred Harvey. Like Allan Pinkerton, he wasn't afraid of hiring women. Why not one for his own in-house security?

So much the better if she was Pinkerton-trained.

# About the Author

DANA STABENOW was born in Anchorage, Alaska and raised on a 75-foot fishing tender. She knew there was a warmer, drier job out there somewhere and found it in writing. Her first book in the bestselling Kate Shugak series, *A Cold Day for Murder*, received an Edgar Award from the Mystery Writers of America.

Contact Dana via her website:
www.stabenow.com